FAKE LIES

Robert Brown Butler

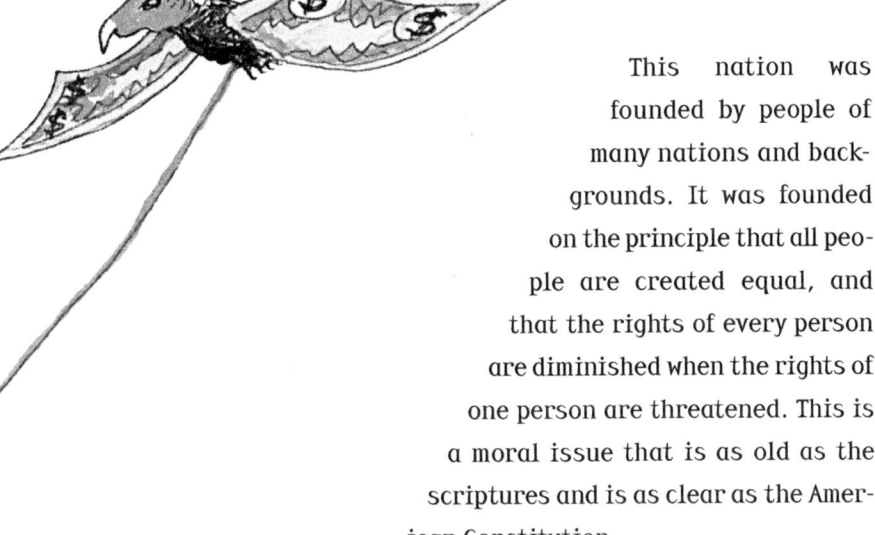

This nation was founded by people of many nations and backgrounds. It was founded on the principle that all people are created equal, and that the rights of every person are diminished when the rights of one person are threatened. This is a moral issue that is as old as the scriptures and is as clear as the American Constitution.

John F. Kennedy

We're talking about a foreign government that, using technical intrusion, lots of other methods, tried to shape the way we think, we vote, we act. That is a big deal. And people need to recognize it. It's not about Republicans or Democrats. They're coming after America, which I hope we all love equally. They want to undermine our credibility in the face of the world. They think that this great experiment of ours is a threat to them, and so they're going to try to run it down and dirty it up as much as possible. That's what this is about. And they will be back, because we remain — as difficult as we can be with each other, we remain that shining city on the hill, and they don't like it.

James B. Comey

OTHER BOOKS BY ROBERT BROWN BUTLER

The Ecological House

Architectural & Engineering Calculations Manual (MH)

Standard Handbook of Architectural Engineering (MH)

Architectural Engineering: Structural Systems (MH)

Architectural Engineering: Mechanical Systems (MH)

Architectural Formulas (MH)

The Power of Babel: BuBabel Typeface User's Guide

Architecture Laid Bare

Disaster Handbook

Write Your Tale Off!

MH = published by McGraw-Hill

A PEEK AT THE AUTHOR

Robert Brown Butler lived in Georgia until he entered Cornell University where he earned a degree in architecture. As an architect and author of numerous architectural engineering books for Mc-Graw-Hill he is a noted authority in his field. He is a dynamic public speaker, and he plans to write ten more books for which he has extensive notes and drafts that he can finish in the near future.

This book is kindly
dedicated to Jim Phillips.
Of the facts and ideas
expressed on these pages
his knowledge has given
them molecular weight.

Though this visual ritual
  may unfold as fiction,
    the stage of scenes and players it lays
    posit an ominous truth:
    A cameo
      that brings into sharp relief
      an aspiring tyrant who would
      obliterate the aesthetics
        of our foundational Constitution
        for his own personal gain.
        Make no mistake:
          The freedoms spelt in our Mother of Laws
          are *more* than emotionally ennobling:
            They foster a prosperous comity
            in our citizenry:
            They bring out the best
              in our single selves
                for the mutual benefit of all.
                End these fortune-feeding freedoms,
                and life as Americans have known it
                for decades will end.

OVERHEARD IN THE OVAL OFFICE

IT IS A SIMPLE STORY, really. A rather short story, one that limns the destiny of a citizenry as it inheres in the hands of one man; and as of the day this tale was penned little occurs in the past. Hence no records stored in dusty files, no myths handed down through the ages, no research performed by diligent scribes, nor any probing of elders' memories for vague remembrances could guide this foray into the frontiers of the future. But we know something will happen by what exists now, as evidenced by overhearing a certain private conversation transpiring in an office known to all....

"...Well that was a nice party we had. Must have been a million out there, all the way to the Washington Monument."

"But Boss, did you see how one network showed the Mall was nearly empty? Lots of lawn where everybody should have been standing."

"I saw that. Said we drew 250,000 people, but it's a lie. A twenty-block area, all the way to the Washington Monument, was packed. Saw it myself."

"The media said you didn't draw near as many people as Obama did his first inauguration."

"Another lie, fake news."

Third voice: "They even showed pictures. Aerial photographs."

"Probably taken when the place was empty. But we finally got that uppity black man outa there. Eight long years...sick."

Fourth voice: "We'll sweep his dead wood out with a heavy broom."

"We'll do it with a dump truck, a fleet of em. We're gonna end it, drain the swamp, beautiful. You see those other presidents there?"

"Yeah."

"Nice company. That Carter must be ninety years old."

Third voice: "Ninety-two."

"Ninety-two years old. Jesus. Maybe after a few cancelled elections I could be still sitting here when I'm that old. Felt good having the Chief Justice — what's his name?"

Fifth voice: "Roberts."

"Roberts. First name please?"

"John. John Glover Roberts."

"John Glover Roberts. Felt good having him hold that Bible under my hand, feeling all that power and money flowing into me like a tidal wave."

Second voice: "Your wife sure looked nice."

"She always looks nice. Very cooperative. How bout a bottle. Not the gold this time, the blue."

"Shoot for the moon, taxpayer's treat. Let's see...six, seven. Wynton, you in on this?"

"All in, Boss."

"Baron, get seven glasses and a bucket of ice from the bar closet." Long pause...sound of a tray set on a desk...glasses clinking...liquid pouring into each glass. "Here's to making America great again."

Several mens' voices cheer.

"Aaah, nothing like blue, especially when it's free."

"It's on the house."

"Right, on the house. One that's big and *white*. Here's to all our black brothers, wherever they are."

Second voice: "Back in Africa where they came from."

The voices cheer.

"And here's to all our Latin amigos, wherever they are."

Second voice: "South of the wall."

The voices cheer.

"And here's to all our Muslim buddies, wherever they may be."

Second voice: "Home where they belong."

The voices cheer.

"Some peace-loving religion they have."

Second voice: "Yeah, they'd love to see a piece of you here, a piece of you there, another piece of you over there."

Laughter.

"Those bastards, I don't trust a one of em. Anyone want another? Here you go Baron. You too Clay. Attaboy."

Fifth voice: "What are we gonna do first, Boss?"

"First we'll make everybody love us."

"Everybody but the media, right?"

"Right. Everyone else, I'll say you are really special, really amazing people, very very few people could have done what you did. Pass out the red caps with our motto by the millions. Make everyone feel great again!"

"Make every little guy feel like a big guy."

"Yeah. Specially those mutts in the Rust Belt. I should send every one of em a bottle of this. Wrap it in a little confederate flag."

"Hey, why don't you give David a call. Thank him for his support."

"Good idea. Where's the phone?"

Second voice: "On the floor under your desk. I put it there when Johnny walked in so you'd have room for the glasses."

"Well put it back up here."

"Anything you say Boss." Sound of the phone being set on the desk.

"Got his number?"

"Right here."

Sound of the phone being dialed. "H'lo…this David? David Duke?"

"…His brother? Big brother or little brother?"

"…The middle one? How many brothers you got?"

"…Four? The others crazy as he?"

"…Peas in a pod, ha haa. Well, keep up the good work. Can you put David on the line?"

"…Tell him it's the President."

"…Of the United States, that's what."

"…No, it isn't a joke. Put your brother David on the line."

"…David? This David Duke?"

"…The President of the United States, that's who it is."

"…Would I lie to you? You know I never lie."

"…Good, beautiful. David my friend, I really appreciate all the support you gave us, you and your people are really special, really amazing people, very very few people could have done what you did. Sorry I can't make my feelings better known publicly, but I'll do everything for your people that I can, and you know my head will be turned when they're running free."

"…We'll make things great all right. Give this country back to the people it was made for."

"…Yeah, Spencer too. When was the last time you talked to Jared?"

"…When you hear from them again, tell them I thank them for their support, their people are really special, really amazing people. More than anyone else, you guys pushed me over the goal line on election day."

"…Good, good. So keep wearing those red caps and trolling for strays."

"…And grab some pussy for me if you get a chance. I'm a little stuck here, can't slip around like I used to. And say goodbye to your brother for me."

"…Okay. Good, good, beautiful."

"…Yeah, will do."

Click of a phone hanging up. "Good man. Wonder how many votes he and his people pulled in for us?"

"Maybe a hundred thousand in Pennsylvania and Ohio and Michigan alone."

"Could be right. Hey, I ought to send David a case of this, taxpayers' treat. Clay? Clay Cockspur? Where'd he go?"

"He's in the head, Boss."

"Well tell him to get his ass back here." Footsteps…long pause…footsteps. "Can't you hold your liquor better than that?"

"It was left over from breakfast, Boss."

"Ha haa. Anyway, send a case of this to my good friend David Duke down in Louisiana. Pack excelsior around each bottle so they won't break. Howland, you have his address?"

Right here Boss.

"Give it to Clay. Clay, take it from here……"

Next Monday morning as President Conan Cain is seated at his desk in the Oval Office, his press secretary enters with the day's *Washington Post* in his hand and a very anxious look on his face. "Boss," pointing to an article on the front page, "You better read this."

The President opens the paper on his desk and looks at the article…

WASHINGTON— Saturday morning after his inauguration the day before,

Conan Cain sat at his desk in the Oval Office with a gathering of his spanieling aides and made his first telephone call as President of the United States.

He made the call to David Duke, the American radical rightist and former Imperial Wizard of the Ku Klux Klan, who lives in Louisiana.

The President's face reddens.

The President reportedly thanked Mr. Duke for his support in winning the election last November. Cain also congenially asked about Richard Spencer, president of the National Policy Institute, a white nationalist think tank, and Jared Taylor, who edits the white supremacist publication American Renaissance, and he asked Duke to thank them for their support. As Cain chatted with his cronies he referred to one of his core constituents, poor young whites who the President said the previous administration left behind, as "mutts".

Manuring this malodorous atmosphere with the President were his Press Secretary, Clay Cockspur; his Chief Strategist and Senior Counselor, Baron Clasher; the White House Chief of Staff, Wynton Mastoguet; Cain's former campaign manager, Howland Thrile; his attorney General, Bricker Soliminus; and his Advisor on Legal Matters, Duey McDougall. The President served everyone glasses of Johnny Walker blue scotch, reportedly costing $190 a bottle, which he offered as "taxpayers' treats". Together this party derisively toasted their "black brothers" saying they would be "back in Africa where they came from," their "Latin amigos" saying they would be "south of the wall," and their "Muslim buddies" saying they would be "Home where they belong—"

"Who's the fucker who leaked this!"

"Boss, not so loud, your secretaries are working down the hall."

"I don't give a shit who's working down the hall, who leaked this to the press!"

"I have no idea."

"The way this is wrote our words were recorded!"

"Maybe it was a plant."

"It sure wasn't some deep throat in a parking garage a few miles away! You get everyone who was in this room then by nine o'clock this morning!"

"Mr. McDougall is in New York this morning, sir."

"Being my advisor on legal matters he's the *first* person I want in here! You tell Duey to set up a video conference from wherever he is in New York to my office by ten o'clock, and I don't give a shit if the Russians have blown up China you get everyone else in here by ten o'clock! I'll find out who did this if I –I –I have to waterboard every one of em!"

The Reds Cross Swords

WHAT COULD POSSIBLY have led to this loathsome episode transpiring in the loftiest office of the land?

It didn't pop out of thin air.

No, it had to evolve from something, some social foundation, some trench of discontent in which was poured the hardening cement of enmity, so easily diverted at first, yet when allowed to cure in the air of unwariness can become as hard to tear down as walls of granite. To see how this loathsome episode evolved, let us trace its advance backward —run the reel of history in reverse at the speed of light— to a certain seed of circumstance from which it perversely bloomed, then slow its growing so we can warily see how each odious moment flowered, with perhaps a ghost hovering in the shadows to aid our enlightening —but enough of idle conjecture! In these respects, the sperm meets the egg in this creepy tale with a gentle knock on a door...

"That must be them," she cries, her voice quivering.

Her husband eyes his watch. Ten till nine. Though he is of middling stature every detail of his appearance is imbued with elegance. His silvery hair is smoothly combed, his deeply set blue eyes seem almost hypnotic, and his lips project slightly as if ready to speak in an instant, all of which would lead one to say, 'I can see why he's a minister.' He enters the foyer, his steps hesitant as if fearing a crisis. As if some strange specter lurks beyond the periphery of his senses: that even in the shelter of his home could invade and conquer him —that even a man of cloth would have little power to repel.

As he nears the door, in the light of the porch light shining through the sidelight aside the door appears a tall shoulder above a jacketed arm and trousered leg. The host sighs as if salvation has arrived. He unlocks the bolt above the knob and eagerly widens the door.

Beyond stands a tall rangy man with thinning white hair, his face slightly bowed and his right hand propped on a cane, and at his side stands a woman whose shoulderlength gray hair frames a gentle face with attentive eyes, a glint of diamond on her left hand. Says the host to the guest, "Hi Hod,"

"Hi Archie. Here we are for the great performance."

"Yes," heaving a thankful sigh. "Come in, come in."

The lady steps first through the door, Hod leaning on his cane following. "Lydia," Archie looks at his wife, "I'd like you to meet Hod Hawksbill and his lovely wife, Jocelyn."

Hod glances at his wife while gesturing a hand toward the hosts, "and this is Reverend Archibald Munch, Archie for short, and his wife, Lydia."

Says Jocelyn, "I've heard *so* many nice things about your sermons, Reverend. You're quite well-known around here."

"Thank you, but the main attraction tonight is your husband." Archie closes the door and relocks the bolt and looks at Hod, "How're you holding up?"

"With the weather as nice as it was today, my knees haven't felt better in weeks. But right now they tell me a storm is coming."

In the confiding warmth inside the door they four converge as if to share a secret, their eyes filled with a glitter hinting the onset of tears. Their eyes interconnect, forming a cerebral link, of reading in their minds a fear that they face a serious danger: one eerily mysterious, one measurelessly remote yet momentously real, one that could mean life as they have known it for decades might —just might— end if a few hundred million people aren't careful; that together they feel stronger, as if in the mind of each reinforcements have arrived. Archie looking at Hod heaves a deep sigh, "I'm glad you could come over. The first one was so crazy, Lydia and I felt we needed someone who knows something about these things to shepherd us through the next one."

"I'll do what I can."

Says Lydia to Hod, "The whole thing frightens me so!" her voice trembling.

"To think that one of them could hold my *life* in their hands! It's scary!"

"We have a lot to be scared about this time around."

"You worked with people like this?"

"I wouldn't say I worked *with* them, but Washington was my beat."

"You were a journalist there?"

Nodding, "For forty-odd years. And some were pretty odd years."

"Is it true that back in the Sixties you attended some of Johnson's press conferences?"

"Dozens of them. I covered the passage of all his Great Society legislation. He was amazing the way he could get senators and congressmen to vote for his bills. Too bad we don't have somebody like him now."

"What was he like?"

"He was big. He was taller than me and I was six-three, and he wasn't fat at all. I'd say he weighed a solid 230, 235 pounds. He had heavy brows and big ears and long jowls that with the way he usually looked down a little made him look like a bloodhound sniffing for a scent. Probably was too. When he walked into a room, you knew he was there."

"After LBJ left office, what'd you do?"

"I was a Senate investigator. For forty years I leaked stories to all the major publications on the East Coast, exposing corrupt and crooked people whenever I could."

"When Nixon and Reagan were presidents too?"

"Yup. Carter, Clinton, both Bushes. In one way or another they made sure I never ran out of work."

"My, my, for forty years. But, isn't leaking –a little, sneaky?"

"I was dealing with sneaky people. But their sneakiness was outside the law while mine was inside the law. When I came across some important information the public had a right to know, I leaked it to a responsible periodical. For forty years I was well known as somebody nobody knew."

"Nobody ever discovered you?"

"Nope, other than I was known as the sieve that lived in the shadows of the swamp."

Archie eyes his watch. "It's nearly nine o'clock. We better hustle." They follow Archie through the hall. Into a cozy den where each settles into a chosen sofa or armchair arranged around a coffeetable covered with platters of finger foods before a wide-screen TV display mounted high on the far wall. Archie lifts the remote before his knees and his thumb presses a few buttons as he aims it at the screen.

The screen blinks —appears a large auditorium gilded with red white and blue bunting, its stage bare and its seats filled with cheering voices. A camera zooms in on a slender blond woman seated at a table in front of the audience and facing the stage. "GOOD EVENING LADIES AND GENTLEMEN," her voice is strong and snappy. "WELCOME TO MOORES OPERA CENTER AT THE UNIVERSITY OF HOUSTON HERE IN HOUSTON, TEXAS. IT IS NINE P.M. ON THE EAST COAST AND THE MOMENT OF TRUTH HAS ARRIVED. THIS IS CARLA HARPWELL, YOUR HOST FOR THE LATEST DEBATE OF THE 2016 REPUBLICAN PRESIDENTIAL CAMPAIGN, WHICH IS NOW UNDERWAY. HERE ARE THE CANDIDATES."

Amid a din of applause the moderator introduces the candidates as they appear one by one. Each gazes at the audience, their hands waving here and there, then they pace across the stage to a row of imposing lecterns, their poised figures in their sleek suits heralding the hope and prosperity they have come to promise the nation tonight.

Yet —might the minds behind these shining faces proclaiming a greater future for all callously wonder if Mr. and Mrs. Voter would remember a similar row of candidates poised before them four, eight, twelve years ago? Who among these contenders for the nation's highest office would dare say before these millions of viewers as they vie for their votes: "I will promise you the world here tonight, only to leave you in the lurch once your ballot has slipped from your grasp. As for the promises I will make in your behalf tonight, if elected, before my term shall end it is more likely that I shall betray you with a kiss, and your hopes will be dashed before they would ever be fulfilled. The adamantine truth? No jobs here. No affordable cares. No opportunities fluttering with cash. Not even clean water in some places. Yes —even more than gladly appearing before you tonight I am glad that your memories, ever diminishing during each fatiguing term of office yet gilded every four years with renewed hope, are so fleetingly short! The pursuit of happiness, yes. The fulfillment of it —hah, another matter!"

As Lydia and Jocelyn sip their drinks and Archie butters a cracker with brie, Hod unnoticingly slips his right hand into the side pocket of his trousers. There, if you would chance to look really close, you could see the fabric above his hand ripple a little. As if a finger beneath is moving a switch.

The applause diminishes and the moderator's voice becomes more conversational. "Tonight, hundreds of people here along with millions of voters at home will have another opportunity to see the Republican candidates for the President of the United States face off in a debate about the most pressing issues concerning the public today. Several months from now, one of these candidates appearing tonight will likely accept their party's nomination for President of the United States. Each candidate will have one minute to answer each question and will be allowed 30 seconds for follow-ups, and if one candidate criticizes another the latter gets a 30-second rebuttal. If a candidate speaks too long, you'll hear this:" *Rinnggg...*"Pleasant, no?

"Now for the evening's first question. Many Americans are concerned about the large number of illegal immigrants entering this country, estimated to be more than a million per year, and their willingness to work for lower wages than American citizens. We start tonight with you, Mr. Conan Caine. Mr. Caine, several weeks ago you announced that if you are elected president, you will build a wall along America's Mexican border to keep them out."

"Yes," his hulking shoulders clad in a dark blue suit lean ominously over the lectern, a shingle of blond hair combed over his forehead like the eave of a roof,"we need to build a wall, a beautiful wall, and it has to be built quickly. Because the Mexican government is sending criminals, murderers, rapists, drug dealers, into this country—

"*False!*" —beside the candidate appears a ghostly figure, a grayish translucency, his silky face and neat attire vaguely visible.

"Who's that!" Archie's eyes bulge at the monitor.

"Shhh," says Hod quietly, "let's hear what it says."

The ghost leans toward the candidate and looks him straight in the eye: "The Mexican government is *not* sending criminals, murderers, rapists, and drug dealers into this country like you said." The words of his tenor voice pop like pistol shots from his mouth.

"Who the hell are you!"

"I'm the truth. The Mexican government isn't doing what you said—"

"They are—"

"They're not—"

"Yes they are. Mexico is sending them. I have statements—"

"You don't have any statements because nobody ever made any! You lie because you think no one watching can quickly dispute what you say. The immigrants enter on their own, and many aren't even from Mexico but arrive from Latin countries further south."

The candidate looks at the moderator. "Who is this guy?"

"I don't know, but he seems to know what he's saying."

The candidate grumps at the ghost, "This subject wasn't even on anybody's mind until I brought it up at my announcement—"

"Another lie! During the last thirty years *The Washington Post* alone has published 21 articles concerning the entry of illegal immigrants in this country. Any viewer who knows the facts can refute your lies in a second!"

"And the Border Patrol, I was at the border last week—"

"You lie again! —you were campaigning in Pennsylvania and North Carolina and Florida all last week."

"The Border Patrol, people I deal with, that I talk to, they say this is what's happening—"

"You never talked to a Border Patrol person in your life—"

"Because our leaders are stupid."

"Another insolent lie. And you call Shillery Mitten a liar!"

"Crooked Shillery?"

"You're twenty times crookeder than she ever was—"

"She lies all the time."

"You're the one who lies all the time."

"I don't lie."

"You did it again!"

"Wrong, wrong—"

"Are you so bullying and dishonest that all you can say is one lie after another in effort to fool a fallible public?"

"And the Muslims, we need to deport them."

"No we don't—"

"Look at what they did to the World Trade Center."

"That was a small group who profaned to be Muslims when millions of devoted Muslims believe in a God of mercy and Love—"

"Wrong, wrong, we should deport every one, millions of em, beautiful."

"If we deported millions of law-abiding Muslims because ten demented ones destroyed the World Trade Center, by your defective logic we should deport millions of law-abiding Christians because a Christian killed 9 worshippers in a church in Charleston last year, a Christian killed 26 children and teachers in a school in Newtown in 2012, a Christian killed 168 government workers in Oklahoma City in 1995, and many more Christians kill hundreds of innocent people in this country every year."

MODERATOR: "I don't know where this person is from, but ladies and gentlemen, it's time to move to another topic." One of the regions of greatest turmoil in the world today is Syria. Several factions have been waging war in that country for five years. Ms. Farley Clorina, as former CEO of a major American corporation, you have experience in dealing with big problems. What would be your strategy for ending the war there?

A slender woman wearing a light blue dress leans her narrow face over the lectern. "To win the war, we need generals who have made tough calls in tough times and stood up to be held accountable over and over. One thing I would immediately do is bring back the warrior class —generals like Petraeus, Mattis, McChrystal, and Keane. Every one of these generals I know—"

"*False!*" —the ghost again! "You never met a one of those generals in your life."

"Of all the…who are you?"

"I'm me."

"Where are you?"

"Looking at you."

"…As I was about to say, every one of those generals was retired early because they told President Obama things he didn't want to hear—"

"Three lies out of four! Three of those generals were *not* retired early by President Obama as you say—"

"Who are you to know!"

"I know General Petraeus *resigned* —wasn't retired— after he shared classified documents with a woman with whom he had an affair. And General McChrystal was publically pressured to leave after making disparaging remarks about Joseph Biden in *Rolling Stone* magazine. And General Keane resigned in 2003 —six years before Obama was even president! You tell such obvious lies because you think no one is here to quickly refute them."

"This network has fact checks."

"Oh, sure. Ninety million viewers listen to you lie and not a million read the fact checks next morning. You fool the public by telling a lie whose words appear so briefly on the screen that viewers can't think about what they heard before you clobber their ears with your next words. If viewers had time to think about each word you say, they'd know you just spoke an outright disgusting knowing blatant baldface lie!"

"Well…I've never been so insulted in my life!"

"It's early yet. If you want to speak the truth about Syria, say any strategy to end the war must begin with knowing five factions are fighting each other there and three are backed by enemies of the United States."

"How do you know all this?"

"By learning it as easily as you could."

MODERATOR: "Well, something's going on here that CNN hadn't planned on! But let's move to another topic. Mr. Rowell Garnett, as a first-term senator, it has been said you are too inexperienced to be President because you have never dealt with the kinds of serious crises you would need to deal with if you were president. What is your response to this?"

Answers a shortish man with a roundish face and youthfully dark hair, "First, let's dispel this fiction that Barack Obama doesn't know what he's doing. He knows exactly what he's doing. He is trying to make America be like the rest of the world. We don't want to be like—"

The ghost again— *"You avoided the question!"*

"What?"

"You avoided the question! The question was not if Barack Obama knows what he is doing, but how would you convince the public that you are experienced enough to be president."

"Excuse me, whoever you are, as I was saying, let's dispel this fiction that Barack Obama doesn't know what he's doing. He knows exactly—"

"You did it again! You're saying what Washington trains politicians to say: Avoid the issue with a drive-by shot that kills peoples' attention then you give the memorized twenty-second sound bite your handlers give you. When you're President, citizens don't want to hear a bunch of patriotic platitudes when a crisis occurs; they want you to get the highways cleared, and reopen their stores and their schools, and rebuild their communities. You're doing none of this by avoiding the question."

"Here's the bottom line," the candidate looks straight at the camera. "This notion that Barack Obama doesn't know what he's doing just isn't true. He knows exactly what he's—"

"You're doing it again! The same dumb twenty-second sound bite you gave before and would give again and again. No wonder voters think you'd make a poor president."

"You don't know what you're talking about."

"If I agreed with you we'd both be wrong."

MODERATOR: "Well! I wouldn't have had the moxie to say that. But let's move to another topic, one that concerns millions of women in America. Governor Warren Stalker of Wisconsin, you've said you want to make abortion illegal even in cases of rape or to save the life of the mother. Would you really let a mother die rather than allow her to have an abortion?"

"Well," says a shortish stern man whose pale skin contrasts brightly with his dark suit, "I believe my position is consistent with many Americans—"

"*False*" —the ghost again, "83 percent of Americans favor an exception when the mother's life is at stake.

"What the... whoever you are, I strongly believe in pro-life."

"If you strongly believe in pro-life, what about the mother's life? Pro-life is pro-mother's life as much as pro-fetus's life."

"Sir, due to my strong Christian faith, I believe abortion is evil."

"Fine, there's nothing wrong with believing that, the Constitution says you have a right to believe that —but by this same right the Constitution says you have *no* right to force your religious views on someone whose religion differs from yours. You have no more right to force another to believe your religious views on abortion than a Navaho has the right to make you believe Spider Woman is a consort of the Sun God. The Constitution says our government should have *nothing* to do with religions, other than to keep any citizen from forcing one's religious views on another."

"The Constitution says I'm free to do as I feel."

"Free *to* also means free *from*. Your freedom to do as you feel ends when you violate the freedom of others. Your freedom to swing your fist ends where another's nose begins."

"My freedom includes reading the Bible, which says killing a baby before it's born is murder."

"Nowhere does the Bible says abortion is murder."

"How do you know?"

"I know Genesis 2:7 says, "The Lord God formed man by breathing into his nostrils the breath of life and man became a living soul." The Bible —*your* Bible— says a person's life begins not at conception or any measure of fetal growth but when they begin to breathe —when they are born."

"Other Bible verses say otherwise. They say abortion is *wrong*, and any woman who has one and anyone who helps her ought to be thrown in jail."

How would you like it if a few pro-choicers came to you and said due to your wrongful views on abortion we're going to throw *you* in jail! They don't want to send you to prison, they don't want to attack you with deadly weapons or vandalize your property as some pro-lifers do, they just want to be left alone to do what they believe is best. Here the real issue isn't abortion; it's *repression*: prohibiting another's free rights which violates the Constitution."

"But taxpayers who don't believe in killing babies shouldn't have to pay for women to have abortions."

"Taxpayers pay for only 24 percent of abortions."

"That's a quarter of a million a year."

"Regardless of the number, each one would cost taxpayers a lot less than paying for the baby's birth, plus post-natal care, plus welfare checks and food stamps for indigent mothers, plus social counseling and child care for possibly several years. These are the *facts*, and any politician who tries to steal someone's vote by duping them due to their religious views is breaking the law —and *they're* the ones who should be thrown in jail."

Moderator: "Well! We have exceeded the allowed time, so let's move to another topic…"

For two hours the debating wages on, the candidates thrusting and parrying on a battlefield a nation wide, the "ghost" correcting the candidates' every inaccuracy, every misleading, and every lie with impeccable logic and unquestionable fact.

Finally ends the debate. "Wheeew…!" Archie lifts the remote from the coffeetable before his knees and blackens the screen. He looks at Hod, "that ghost sure put those bunglers in their place! I can't tell you the times a candidate has said something I *knew* was wrong, and I wish I could have stood right next to them and said what he said. Who do you think he was?"

"Beats me," Hod lies, his hand slipping unnoticingly into his trouser's pocket. "But since you're a minister, I'd like to ask you about something that ghost said."

"What's that?"

"When he quoted a Bible verse that says a baby's life begins when it begins to breathe, when it is born, and that politician said other Bible verses say otherwise. What do you know about this?"

"Well, a few Bible verses do speak of the sanctity of life in the womb. For example, Jeremiah 1:5 says God knows us before He forms us in the womb."

"But if God knows us before He forms us in the womb, this could mean He knows us if our parents discussed having us months before they conceived, and that wouldn't have determined when our lives began."

"…A valid point. But Psalm 139:13 also speaks of God's active role in our creation and formation in the womb."

"But that says nothing about whether the baby was alive in the womb, only that God is actively involved in its development before it is born."

"Another valid point. But there's another Bible verse that would shed some light on this. In Exodus 21, just after Moses received the command-ments."

"Do you know what it says?"

"Not exactly. It's rather long."

"You have a Bible around here?"

"I have several."

"Why don't you get one and let's see what it says?"

"Would you like King James or the Modern Version?"

"Ooh, let's look at King James."

Archie steps from the room and moments later returns with a Bible and sits back down and opens it on his knees. "Let's see..." turning some pages. "Here, Exodus 21, verse 22: "'If men strive, and hurt a woman with child, so that her fruit depart from her, and yet no mischief follow, he shall be surely punished, according as the woman's husband will lay upon him; and he shall pay as the judges determine.'"

"Well...I can see how a pro-lifer would side with that. But again, those words can be interpreted another way."

"How's that?"

"If the man who departs the fetus from the woman is a doctor, and he does it with the husband's and the woman's permission, then no mischief should follow, and the only pay a judge would determine is the doctor's fee for the operation. Again, two interpretations of the same words, and anyone has a right to believe either interpretation as they want and has no right to make others believe the same."

"Hmm. Genesis 2, verse 7. I can feel a sermon being born about this."

"What a novel idea. A minister influencing the public about a religious issue." Hod pauses in thought. "Here's another idea for a sermon. The ghost said the real issue behind all this isn't abortion; it's *repression*: prohibiting another's free rights which violates the Constitution."

"Come to think of it, the Constitution says several kinds of repression are unlawful. Repression of free speech, religion, women voting, blacks —all unlawful. Together they could say, Thou shalt not repress thy neighbor."

"Maybe that should be the eleventh commandment."

"Maybe it should be the first one."

"Yeah. Think of all the repressive ways a politician tries to win votes. A politician may know nothing about domestic issues and even less about foreign issues —but if he yells *I'm pro-life*, millions will vote for him for that one reason alone, and they'll pull that trick anytime they think they can gain more votes than they'll lose by wrongfully slamming Latinos, Muslims, blacks, reds, yellows, gays, any group whose numbers are less than their core."

"Voters fall for that trick all the time."

"Yeah, the wolf only slathers at the sight of more sheep. As I sniff the prevailing winds on what we saw tonight, I don't see any good coming of it."

Lydia eyes her watch. "My, it's eleven thirty, and I have to work tomorrow." Suppressing a yawn, she looks at her husband. At Hod, at his wife. "Hod, thank you *so* much for coming over and helping us understand these things, and Jocelyn, it's always nice to see you again. The next Democratic debate is two Sundays from now. Would you like to come again?"

Next morning Hod says to Jocelyn, "I need to buy some things in town. Anything we need at CVS or the A&P?"

"Ooh, toothpaste? Bananas maybe? See what milk is in the fridge."

Due to something else on his mind Hod forgets to see what milk is in the fridge and opening the kitchen back door sees the car in the garage. He steps toward the driverside door. Opens it, slides behind the wheel.

He drives into town.

Past CVS.

Past the A&P.

Turns left onto a narrow tree-lined street passing through a venerable neighborhood of tidy red brick bungalows with white trim and narrow porches across their fronts. Without looking at any names or numbers on any passing mailboxes he parks in front of a house on the right that looks much like any other along the street. Cane in hand, he steps not toward the front door but onto the driveway along the house's side, his tender knees making him look like he's stepping daintily over a bed of hot coals. "Ought to use two canes," mumbling, "but damned if I want to look that old." At the house's back corner he turns right. Steps slowly across a patch of lawn. Up to a small door nearly hidden in a tangle of vines sprawling over the back of the house. His right hand propped on his cane, his left hand lifts to the door...

nuk nuk

A long minute later the door slits open an inch. Appears a suspicious eye in an elderly face. The eye brightens, the door widens. In the opening appears a rather disheveled old man who couldn't be more than five feet tall. The red-and-black flannel shirt he wears looks rumpled and dusty, his face is etched with wrinkles and above his left eye appears a large port-wine birthmark, and the top of his head beneath a few wisps of snowy hair is spotted with moles. Not exactly Hollywood's idea of a leading man. But below his frosty eyebrows dance a pair of friendly eyes. "Hi Hod, had an idea you'd stop by," the words of his tenor voice pop like pistol shots from his mouth. "Come in."

The little man turns into a narrow dark hall behind the door and his slippered feet whisper down the hall, Hod a cane-aided step behind. At an open door aglow with light on the left the little man turns into a bedroom-size area against whose left, back, and right walls extends a long U-shaped desk-high counter made of bare plywood, the walls above arrayed with all kinds of computer equipment. Before the counter on the left sits a swivel armchair in front of a computer keyboard, a mug of coffee and a clipboard on the left and a mouse perched on a pad on the right, and to the right of the mouse a large tablet of drawing paper...along the counter's back, two more keyboards, several coffee mugs filled with pencils and magic markers, clutters of other office objects...mounted on the wall above, three large-screen LCD displays with small scribbled notes taped to their black frames...rising above the counter's far corner, the derrick-like base of an architectural drafting lamp whose conical reflector delivers a soft gentle light about the room. Along the counter in back rest several iPads of different colors, one upside-down with its back removed, its filamentous electronics glistening in the ambient light, a tiny screwdriver and a small soldering gun close by...stacked high against the wall behind, dozens of old desktop computers and laptops with wires dangling from them everywhere…shoved under the counter, a cushioned barstool between several scuffed metal tool boxes set on the floor. Opened on the counter to the right is a notebook-size product catalog beside a conference speaker phone, a row of thick product catalogs lining the wall in back…paving the wall above, taped notes, thumbtacked political cartoons, sketchy drawings, other items of personal interest…to the right of the phone, a Mr. Coffee maker, its squatty glass pitcher half-filled with brew next to a huddle of coffee mugs, a box of filters, sugarbowl, jar of powdered cream, stack of paper napkins and a plastic spoon laid on the counter…fitted under the counter beneath the coffeemaker, a small refrigerator. No windows, no other doors, the room silent as a tomb, void of any odor but the faint musk of dusty computers. Everything looking cluttered and disarranged —all indications of a highly organized mind. Behind the soldering gun on the back counter something catches Hod's eye. "An Apple Newton. Haven't seen one of those in years."

"Strange how it died when it was ahead of its time. Hope the same doesn't happen to us." The little man sits in the armchair before the center LCD display and slides the keyboard in front of his little belly and reaching to his right tilts the drafting lamp a little to throw more light on the keys, then without looking over his left shoulder he holds his left hand up to Hod as if he knows why he came.

Hod removes from his trousers' side pocket a strange object looking something like a large bumblebee and sets it in the little man's hand.

He fondly looks at it. "Wi-fi is magic stuff, isn't it?"

"Coming from you it is. I'm amazed it lasted so long."

"Ah, it's only a transmitter," weighing it in his hand, "its power comes from over there," he points to a rack of UPS-like componentry under the counter on his right."

"It's amazing how well it worked."

"Ah, once you know the electronics the rest is little more than formatting, though everything looks better if you can draw, that's where the illusion of reality enters the scene." He reaches for the coffee by the keyboard and takes a sip, as if only a few drops of this additive every few minutes is all the energy the four-cylinder engine chassis'd in his chest needs to keep chugging and sets the mug down. "You want to program it again?"

Hod nods. "See if you can set it for the Democratic debate two Sundays from now."

"Got a time and date?"

"March sixth, I think. Try nine o'clock."

"Let's look at the channel directory." The little man's right hand slides the mouse over the pad as his left fingers tap the keys. On the center display above the counter appears a program with columns of names, titles, times. The program scrolls down. "There we go...nine P.M." His little fingers flit about the keys. "Shillery's more complicated though. Instead of blurting baldface lies about a subject she warbles around it without ever getting to the point. 'Liar,' Cain calls her. She's not too bright, but she's a saint of truth compared to him. And that blowhard senator who keeps hounding her, he exaggerates every fact and interrupts people when they're talking and won't shut up until the moderator cuts him off." He heaves a sigh. "In some of the longer passages last night it was touch and go. I'll beef this up a little. See what kind of political brain surgery we can perform this time. Can you wait a half hour?"

Hod eyes his watch. "I can buy some things at CVS and the A&P."

THE BLUES CROSS SWORDS

GOOD EVENING EVERYONE," booms the moderator, "THIS IS BARON STRIKER FROM WHITING AUDITORIUM IN FLINT, MICHIGAN. TONIGHT CBS NEWS BRINGS YOU THE LATEST DEBATE BETWEEN THE TWO MAJOR DEMO-CRATIC CANDIDATES FOR THE PRESIDENT OF THE UNITED STATES." The applause diminishes and the moderator's voice becomes conversational. "On the left is former Secretary of State, Shillery Mitten...

Applause...

On the right, the Senator from Vermont, Brian Dansser...

Applause...

Tonight these two candidates will answer questions about how they would deal with some of the crucial issues facing America today if they were President. As moderator," looking at the camera, "I'll set some ground rules. I'll ask the candidates the questions, then I'll ask for follow-ups where appropriate and guide the discussion. The rules for tonight's debate are simple. One minute for answers, 30 seconds for follow-ups, and if one candidate criticizes another the latter gets a 30-second rebuttal. If a candidate speaks too long, I will end discussion on that topic and proceed to the next.

We will begin with former Secretary of State Shillery Mitten. Secretary Mitten, considering the spread of ISIS throughout the Near East, a controversial issue today is that America wrongfully invaded Iraq after 911. Since you originally voted to invade Iraq then later said your vote was a mistake, what is your opinion of this?"

"Well," her rouged face framed by her stylishly cropped dark blond hair tilts toward the lectern, "first of all, immediately after 911, in the White House and on Capital Hill there was a lot of political pressure to invade Iraq, and there was a lot of loose talk going on there—"

—Appears the ghost: "*There's a lot of loose talk going on here.*"

"Pardon me," looking surprised…"who are you?"

"I'm me. Instead of warbling around the question get to the point: Why did you initially vote to invade Iraq and later say your vote was a mistake?"

"As I was about to say, when President Bush said Saddam Hussein had weapons of mass destruction in that country, I believed we should remove them, but after we didn't find any of those kinds of weapons there, I said we shouldn't have invaded Iraq."

"Don't beat around the Bush, say he *lied* to Congress that Hussein had those weapons, and when you learned he lied you said your vote was a mistake. The more incisive you are the more intelligent you'll look."

"Sir, I believe I know more about this issue than any other candidate running for president."

"Then *show* it. If you know more about this issue than any other candidate, say what none of them has said, that the spread of ISIS throughout the Near East began in Iraq after our toppling of Hussein created a power vacuum there and —most important— *this happened when Bush was president*, not later during Obama's term as the Republicans constantly claim. Here you could score an important point with the voters but you don't."

"Sir, after being a senator for six years and Secretary of State another four years, I believe I've proved I have the tenacity and the track record and the ability to make the best choice for the American people."

"The only tenacity and track record you've proved you have so far is endlessly warbling around a question without answering it, which says little of your ability to make the best choice for anyone."

"Well, I have more experience in these matters than any other candidate."

"If you have more experience in these matters than any other candidate, say what none of them has said or can say, "Are you better off today than you were eight years ago?" This would also align you with a major achievement of your party the last eight years, but you've never said this."

MODERATOR: "With that, let's move to a related topic. Presently America is spending over $600 billion a year on the military, yet in the past few years ISIS has made significant inroads in the near East. Senator Dansser, if you were President, what would you do about this?"

"I would do a lot," his balding head of wispy white hair leans over the lectern, his large glasses looking like goggles and his mouth open as if he's out of breath. "First, we need major reform in the military to make it more cost-effective. We are spending hundreds of billions of dollars maintaining 5,000 nuclear weapons—"

—The ghost again: "*Stick to the subject and don't exaggerate the facts!* First answer the question, which is what would you do about ISIS in the Near East? Second, we don't spend nearly hundreds of billions of dollars maintaining our nuclear weapons alone and we only have 4,000."

"Who are you?" his gogglelike glasses seem to stick out of his head and his jaw drops even lower.

"The Truth. Don't exaggerate the facts! Exaggeration misinforms as much as lies, and voters won't know what to vote for if they're misinformed."

"I do not exaggerate the facts."

"You did it again! You think the voters are idiots?"

"They'll vote for the bills I want to get passed."

"Only gullible voters would believe your fairytale bills would ever be passed by a Republican congress."

"I've accomplished a lot with Republican congresses."

"You've accomplished *nothing* with Republican congresses."

"In the 1990s when I had the Republican leadership—"

"As your state's junior senator and a Democrat you *never* had the Republican leadership of Congress."

"I co-founded the Congressional Progressive Caucus."

"They were left-wing Democrats who had nothing to do with Republicans. Another outrageous exaggeration easily refuted by the facts."

MODERATOR: "Mr. Senator, I'm afraid we've run out of time."

"I haven't had a chance to answer the question."

MODERATOR: "Then go ahead, quickly, Mr. Senator."

"I would do a lot about ISIS in the Near East. First we need major reform in the military to make it more cost-effective—"

The ghost— *"You're repeating what you already said."*

MODERATOR: "Mr. Senator, you really have run out of time, so in all fairness to everyone let's move to another topic. Senator Mitten, next week you are going to testify before Congress about your using a private e-mail server while working at the Department of State. For the last several months you haven't been able to put this issue behind you. You've dismissed it, you've joked about it, you've called it a mistake. What does this say about your ability to handle important issues as president?"

"Well, I've taken responsibility for it."

—The ghost again: *"Don't say something that makes you look clumsy!* Instead say something like, 'The Russians were surprised when they learned I was sending classified information on my private server while they were hacking our regular accounts. What I did was clever and in the best interests of our country.' An answer like this would make you look competent and patriotic instead of stupid and traitorous as the Republicans constantly claim."

"Sir, my personal email use complied with all federal regulations."

"The issue isn't what you did but how you did it. And when Cain insists that you publicly release your emails you could say, 'Since they contain classified information they can't be released to the public.' Voters would understand this and think better of you."

"Sir, there were other kinds of messages, and there's a lot more about this you don't know."

"Such as every president beginning with Reagan has sent classified information in their private emails? Is this not true?"

"...It is true."

"Why don't you *tell* us? If voters knew other presidents did this they'd think better of you doing it. The more you believe that the less the voters know about this issue the better off you'll be, the worse off you'll be."

MODERATOR: "Well, it's obvious who's the cleverest tongue on this stage. But it is time to move on. Senator Dansser, you have often said the greed of Wall Street is hurting our economy. Would you please elaborate on this?"

"Yes. The greed of Wall Street has helped to destroy our economy—"

"*False!*" —the ghost again. "Our economy has greatly improved since 2008—"

"And the lives of millions of people. Check the record."

"The record says the Dow Jones Average has nearly doubled since 2008. Quit making outrageous exaggerations that don't fit the facts."

"I do not exaggerate."

"There you go again, Mister Senator."

"You want a fact? Since 2007 Shillery Mitten and her husband have made 148 million dollars, much of it from giving speeches and doing favors for her greedy cronies on Wall Street!"

Mitten: "Excuse me Mr. Senator, my husband and I paid 48 million of those dollars in federal income taxes. That fact is public record. I'd like to see what taxes Conan Cain has paid on the billions of dollars he claims he has made. As for the speeches I gave, I'm sure that you, Mister Senator, would have gladly accepted those fees if you had been able enough to earn them."

MODERATOR: "But Secretary Mitten, in all candor, how can you convince the nation's voters that you will regulate Wall Street when you may be indebted to its biggest players?"

"Well, you know, both Bill and I have been very blessed. Neither of us came from wealthy families, and we've worked really hard our entire lives—"

—The ghost again: "Quit saying how blessed you are and answer the question! How would you regulate Wall Street when you may be indebted to its biggest players?"

"As I was about to say, I want to make sure that every single person in this country has the same opportunities to make the most of their God-given potential that Bill and I have had—"

"More wimpy warbling! Tell the voters how you'll regulate Wall Street when you're indebted to its biggest players?"

"Well, I, I think it's pretty clear they know I will."

"It's *not* clear. They can't know something you never told them."

"Well, two billionaire hedge fund managers have started a super PAC, and they're advertising against me in Iowa as we speak. So they clearly think I'm going to do what I say I'll do."

"Don't tell us what somebody hundreds of miles away is advertising with a bunch of fuzzy words like 'clearly think', 'going to do', and 'say I'll do' —tell us what *you, right here,* will *definitely* do."

"Sir, in the senate I introduced legislation to reign in excessive pay to banking executives."

"Is that why twenty U.S. banks paid more than two billion dollars in performance bonuses to their top five executives the past four years?"

"And I specifically said to Wall Street that what they were doing in the mortgage market was bringing our country down."

"You *said* something —you didn't *do* anything."

"Well, I've laid out a very aggressive plan to reign in Wall Street and not just the big banks."

"What's your plan."

"And I am going right at them."

"*How* are you going right at them?"

"Well, I've got a tough, five-point economic plan that looks at the whole problem that is praised by a lot of folks."

"What are its five points and what folks are praising it?"

"My plan is more comprehensive than anything else that's been put forth."

"*What is it!* Give its one two three four five points so voters can talk about them around their kitchen tables."

"They're listed on my website. The voters can read them there."

"Read them here! In all the time you've wimpily warbled around this question you could have read them twice!"

MODERATOR: "Well! On that note it's time to move to another topic. An important campaign issue to many Americans is health care. While President Obama was in office he determinedly passed the Affordable Health Care Act. Many believe it is anything but affordable, others praise it for the relief it has brought, and others believe it should be improved. Senator Dansser, what is your policy on health care?"

"In the wealthiest country in the history of the world, we should have affordable health care, truly affordable health care, for every man, woman, and child. That is my goal. And we can make health care affordable for all Americans by breaking up the greedy banks and heavily taxing the hedge fund managers and other rich people with large incomes—"

—Again the ghost: "Quit beating on the banks and the rich and answer the question!"

"Because Wall Street today has enormous economic and political power, and to save our economy the major banks must be broken up—"

"What's this got to do with health care—"

"And we must heavily tax the hedge fund managers and other rich—"

"Quit dodging the question!"

"And I will eliminate the outrageous loopholes that allow multinational corporations to stash billions of dollars in the Cayman Islands and Bermuda and pay zero federal income tax—"

"Gusts of bluster blowing from nowhere to nowhere —what's your policy on health care?"

"That yes, now it is time to see that every man, woman, and child in America has truly affordable health care."

"*Tell us what it is!*"

In fact, it's true, I have introduced a plan for single-payer health care that will be completely paid for by our federal government."

"False! A respected economist, Kenneth Thorpe of Emory University, says your health plan's cost would create a financial shortfall of more than a trillion dollars a year. Another ex-staggeration meant to steal citizens' votes. And how would you get your fairytale bill passed by a Republican Congress?"

MODERATOR: "Mr. Senator, once again your time is up—"

"I haven't described my plan for single-payer health care."

"But your time is up, Mr. Senator, your time is up. So let's move to the next question. Secretary Mitten, an estimated 11 million undocumented immigrants live in this country today. If you are elected President, what would be your policy on immigration reform?"

"Well, we definitely need comprehensive immigration reform. We need to give these people a path toward citizenship, we need to take them out of the shadows. First of all, I would make sure every child gets health care. That's why I helped to create the Children's Health Insurance Program—"

Again the ghost— "Don't brag about something you did that has nothing to do with the question."

"Sir, we need to support states that are expanding health care and—"

"The question isn't about health care it's about immigration reform!"

"Well, you know, I came to Las Vegas in, I think, in early May, and I met with a group of DREAMers. I wish everyone in America could meet with these young people, to hear their stories, to know their incredible talent, their determination—"

"Quit your dithering and get to the point: What's your POLICY on immigration reform?"

"Well –well, you know –first we need to understand that our country is stronger in every generation by the arrival of new immigrants. I mean, we are a nation of immigrants, and today there are many undocumented—"

"Answer the question!"

"Well, we owe a lot to immigrants, and the least we can do is assist the ones who have recently entered this country, to get them on their feet—"

"Get on *your* feet! Tell us your policy on immigration reform?"

"And there is such a difference between everything you're hearing here on this stage and what we hear from the Republicans."

"On this stage we're hearing nothing from you! Give us your policy on immigration reform?"

"Well, my plan would provide instate college tuition to undocumented immigrants."

"So you believe undocumented immigrants should receive instate college tuition."

"Yes, and my policy would support any state that takes that position,

"How would it support it?"

"And I would work with those states,"

"*How* would you work with them?"

"And encourage more states to do the same thing."

"*How* would you encourage them? You're getting in deeper verbal debt with every word you speak!"

"Well, if their states agree, we would want more to do the same thing."

"What if they *don't* agree? Then you have nothing! You could lose this election if you weary voters with empty words."

MODERATOR: "On that note, it's time to move to another topic. Senator Dansser, you have often said you want to offer free tuition in public colleges and universities. How would you do this?"

"Yes. It's not just that college graduates shouldn't be $50,000 or $100,000 in debt, it's that there are students who are in the sixth grade or the eighth grade whose families don't have a lot of money, who aren't even thinking about going to college because they believe it is another world, and I want kids in Burlington, Vermont, and Biloxi, Mississippi, whose families—"

—Again the ghost: "Cut the bluster and answer the question. How would you offer free tuition to students enrolled in public universities?"

"Whose parents, like my parents may never have gone to college, to know that if they study hard and do their homework—"

"How would you offer tuition to students in public universities—"

"That regardless of the income of their families, they are going to be able to get a college education without being $50,000 or $100,000 in debt."

"How would you do this?"

"Now I know some people think it's a radical idea, I don't, I believe that every public college and university in this country should be tuition-free."

"Tell us how you would do it—"

"And it will give hope to millions of young people."

"Hope alone won't lower a tuition bill—"

"Because our campaign is about asking people to think big, not small—
Answer the question!"

"We've got to ask ourselves a simple question, how is it that hundreds of thousands of bright young people today can't go to college because they—"

"Tell us your plan, and how you would get a Republican congress to vote for it."

MODERATOR: "Senator, your time is up, so let's move on to a—"

"I haven't answered the question."

"You remember the question?"

"The question was, uh —could you repeat the question?"

"Mr. Senator, if you can't remember the question, it is time to move on. Secretary Mitten, at a meeting last Spring with a group of businessmen in West Virginia one of them said, and I quote, "We have many friends in this state whose families have worked in the coal mines for generations, and we don't like you saying you want to close the mines." And you said, "You didn't understand what I meant to say." What did you really mean to say?"

"Well, I, what I meant to say was the coal mines are dangerous, and they should be closed until they and the environments around them are safe."

—The ghost again: "What an opportunity you lost! You could have said, 'With proper planning we can keep the mines open while at the same time we can make them and their local environments safer for your friends and families to live and work in.' Right there you lost that state's electoral votes when you could have won them."

"Well, the people working there are suffering."

"Closing the mines on them would only replace their suffering from poor working conditions to suffering from lost work."

"And due to my experience in government I know how to help them."

"We know how helpful your experience in government can be."

"Sir, I have been to West Virginia, I campaigned there for several days, I have seen for myself how much help these people need."

"If you saw so much during your several days there, what kind of help would you give them that would let them keep their jobs *and* improve their working and living conditions? Say something positive here."

"Well– well, you know, the miners, their families, they're poor, they're deprived, their children often don't have enough to eat, even clean water to drink, their lands are ravaged—"

"How would you actually *help* them?"

"Well, we need to go to their communities, and find ways for them to create better lives."

"What are the ways! Wimpy answers won't win votes."

MODERATOR: "Again, I'm afraid that we have run out of time, so let's move on to another topic that concerns many Americans. In nearby Detroit, the public schools have become a national symbol of neglect and failure. It is reported they have issues with rats, mold, broken toilets and water fountains, non-certified teachers, and lack of accountability regarding transportation and special education. Even then this school system is $3.5 billion in debt. In our audience tonight we have Monica Kemp, whose twelve-year-old daughter Richale is a student in Detroit. Monica Kemp is one of ten parents suing Detroit public schools, not for money, she says, but to improve the conditions there. My question will go to both of you, but first to Senator Dansser. What would you do to end these intolerable conditions in Detroit's schools, and other schools where these conditions may exist across the nation?"

"Well, Monica Kemp, thank you for not being resigned to that horrendous situation, but standing up and fighting back. That's what we need all over this country. And, let me be honest with you, hard thing to say, but it is true, a great nation is judged not by how many billionaires it has—"

"Quit beating on the billionaires" —the ghost again— "and answer the question!"

"But how it treats the most vulnerable among us, our children, and the elderly; and you know what—"

"Forget the elderly and stick to the children—"

"We should be ashamed of how we treat our kids and senior citizens—"

"Stick to the kids! What would you do to improve Detroit's schools?"

"We have a Republican leadership in congress now fighting for hundreds of billions of dollars in tax breaks for the top two-tenths of one percent—"

"Forget the rich and stick to the schools!"

"But somehow we can't come up with the money to fix Detroit's crumbling public school system. Somehow we can't make sure that Detroit has qualified and good teachers. Somehow we can't provide summer programs and after-school programs for your children. Somehow we can't do what other countries around the world are doing—"

"Enough of what we *can't* do. What can *you* do?"

"We have got to change our national priorities, no more tax breaks for billionaires and large corporations, then we'll use those taxes to invest in our public schools, and we'll have the best public school system in the world."

"You're repeating the same fairytale babble you said before."

MODERATOR: "Secretary Mitten, how would you help schools like the ones in Detroit?"

"Well, here is how I would help as President. Number one, I would reinstate a program we had during the 1990's where the federal government provided funding to repair and modernize public schools, because a lot of communities can't afford to do that on their own. Secondly, I would use every legal means at my disposal to try to force the Governor and the state to return the schools to the people of Detroit, to end the emergency management, which, I believe, if you look at the data, the situation has only gotten worse with these emergency managers who have put the system further in debt. Number three, I would set up inside the Department of Education, for want of a better term, kind of an education SWAT team, if you will, where we've got qualified people, teachers, principals, maybe folks who are retired, maybe folks who are active, but all of whom are willing to come and help. I also would look at how we could, through the federal government, support more teachers because we're going to have a teacher shortage in some of the hardest-to-teach districts."

Says the ghost, "For once you articulated a feasible plan."

"Yes, thank you. You know, I am proud to have been endorsed by the AFT and the NEA, and I've had very good relationships with both unions, with their leadership. And we've had really candid conversations—"

"Cut the dithering and quit while you're ahead."

"And we need to help our children obtain better educations in our nation's public—"

Interrupts Senator Dansser: "I also believe every public college and university in this country should be tuition free—"

—The ghost: "You interrupted her in the middle of a sentence."

"So if your child regardless of your family's income studies hard, she'll be able to get a college education without being $50,000 or $100,000 in debt—"

"You had your chance!"

"And we should invest in child care—"

"You're not even sticking to the subject."

"Right now you've got child-care workers making McDonald's wages, that is crazy—"

"You don't want her to look better than you!"

"I want well trained, well paid, child care workers to give our youngest kids the most opportunities for their future—

"Enough, Senator!"

"Because our campaign is about asking people to think big, not small—"

"Enough you limelight hog—"

MODERATOR: "Please, please, Senator, your time is up."

As did ten days before, the debate wages on a battlefield a nation wide, the "ghost" constantly correcting the candidates' every warble, every exaggeration, and every burst of impertinence with impeccable logic and unquestionable fact. Finally says the moderator: "We extend our thanks to the Democratic National Committee, as well as our hosts here at Whiting Auditorium in Flint, Michigan, for making this important event possible. And we want to thank our audience, and the people of Flint, and all of you watching at home. Thank you all. Remember, don't let others decide for you. The power is in your hands, so be sure and vote."

"Whe-ew," Archie lifts the remote from the coffeetable before his knees and blanks the screen. "So," looking at Hod, "what do you think?"

"In all my years of watching these debates, going back to Kennedy facing off against Nixon when I was in college, I've never seen a sorrier bunch of candidates. Not a one, Democrat or Republican, has an intelligent command of the issues and the ability to inspire our citizens to greater heights. Take Kennedy in 1960, and Reagan in 1980. I didn't agree with everything they said, but when I was in Washington I attended many of their speeches and press conferences, and nearly every sentence they spoke was perfectly composed. Perfect grammar. Perfect logic. Statesmanlike demeanor. But none of these candidates with their clumsy grammar, flawed logic, flagrant lies, and avoided questions could even win a high school debate."

The others gleam with agreement.

"Also, Kennedy and Reagan were creative geniuses. During one of Kennedy's press conferences, a journalist asked is there any substance to the allegation that his wealthy father financed his winning the election, and Kennedy quipped, 'My father said he was willing to bankroll a bare majority, but he didn't want to finance a landslide.'"

"He said that?" Lydia gasps.

"Yeah. The audience roared. And during another of his press conferences, a journalist said the Republican National Committee recently adopted a resolution that his administration was a failure, and what did Kennedy think of this, and he joked, 'I'm sure the resolution was passed unanimously.' Quick as a fingersnap, with not a note in front of him."

"My, my," Lydia sighs.

"And during Reagan's debate against Mondale in '84 when he was America's oldest president in history, the moderator asked him if his advanced age would detrimentally affect his ability to serve as President, and he answered, 'In this campaign I will not exploit for political purposes my opponent's youth and inexperience.' Even Mondale laughed, and he later said that's when he knew he had lost the election. If you can charm a foreign head of state or a wily senator or stubborn governor like that, you'll accomplish a lot more of what you want. Can you imagine any of this bumper crop of dummies persuading somebody like Mikhail Gorbachev to dismantle the Soviet Union?"

Says Lydia, "I can imagine them dismantling the United States."

"And," says Archie, "at times they were so hateful. If some are so evangelical, why don't they practice what Matthew 5:44 preaches: 'Love your enemies, and bless them that curse you?' And Cain, instead of wanting to wall out the Mexicans and deport the Muslims, he should heed what Mark 12:31 says: 'Thou shalt love thy neighbor as thyself.' Also, Cain made a lot of his money in casinos, but gambling is a sickness. Anyone fit to be our nation's moral leader should try to heal such people, not prey on their weaknesses."

"Another thing," Hod adds. "If you've ever traveled in a war-torn country and seen cities bombed to rubble and rotting with bodies swarming with flies and rats, and the survivors have no food, no clean water, no electricity, no hospitals or doctors or nurses or medications, and no heavy equipment to clear the streets of debris and bury the dead or even any fuel to operate them, and little way for the survivors to organize and make administrative decisions, you would see what bad governing could do in this country."

"It breaks your heart," says Jocelyn.

"Yes, and no humanitarian aid, because when another region is devastated America goes in and helps them, but if we're the ones who are devastated who will help us? And the survivors can't escape if the surrounding lands are defended by the enemy, who before they left often planted mines in the streets and blew up the powerplants which would take months to repair."

"It's scary," says Lydia.

"It sure is. And if you think back at how it all came apart, that sometimes only a couple weeks ago everyone was living comfortably in their homes and neighborhoods, buying food and whatever else they needed in stores and markets nearby, watching TV game shows in the evenings, taking showers every day as if it all would last forever. Then suddenly an imagined slight here, a harsh word there, recriminations, escalations, terrorist attacks, invasions…" Hod bows his head. "Remember how World War I started?" he looks around. "With one person being shot! That's history for you. And when I think of how a year from now one of these dummies might be sitting in the Oval Office, with one hand signing bills we don't need and repealing bills we do need and his other hand on the nuclear button, it sends a chill up my spine."

CAN'T WE DO ANYTHING?

ARCHIE," LYDIA LOOKS UP from her eggs on toast, "the phone."

"I bet I know who it is." He glumly steps to the console and reads the message pane. "Sure enough," pressing the loudspeaker button and leaning toward the console, "Hi Archie."

"Hi Hod. Guess you heard."

"Yeah. The Monster beat the Wimp!"

"Lydia and I tossed and turned all night. He insults women, Muslims, Latinos, even veterans, refuses help from wealthy Republican donors, and loses the debates with Mitten, and still he wins."

"It's amazing what can be done by millions of ignorant people. But he didn't win, Shillery lost. She was a deplorable candidate who gave us Cain on a silver platter. She made so many blunders during her campaign, it's surprising the election was close."

"Makes you wonder how she even won the nomination."

"At least that's explainable. For twenty-five years she's wanted to be America's first woman president, during which she curried favor with the Democratic National Committee until by convention time she could almost run it by herself. She almost drove away with the 2008 nomination until that eloquent upstart from Illinois rear-ended her. But if she had any political brains, long ago she would have given a decent reason why she used a private e-mail server at State and would have had a meaningful economic message for the country. Actually, the one thing that tipped me off about her more than anything else was in one of the emails that —that F.B.I. Director, what's his name?"

"Valley. Clarion Valley."

"Right, had a senior moment there, in one of her emails that Valley investigated, a colleague of hers said her political instincts were sub-optimal. One of her own friends said that."

"She still might have won if Valley hadn't found those emails right before the election."

"But it wasn't the emails that hurt her so much as they were linked to Anthony Weiner, one of the scummiest politicians around. Those emails mated her with as trashy a pussy snatcher as Cain, and a few sleazy remembrances of her husband's impeachment didn't help. Speaking of Bubba, what a blunder he made meeting with Attorney General Lynch on that plane last June! That let Valley step into the batter's box, where with one long drive to the bleachers he sent her to the showers."

"So Cain didn't win, Mitten lost."

"Right. But they weren't the only choices we had. Two other candidates were on the ballot we could have voted for. If 70 million people in this country had wised up about this, right now we might have a better president. So in a way we have only ourselves to blame, including me and you."

"I'll think about that the next time around."

"Me too. But Cain isn't out of the woods yet. Aside from a passionate core group, few people like him. Half the public didn't vote because they didn't like him, over half of those who did vote cast their ballots for Shillery or the other candidates because they didn't like him, and probably half who voted for him did because either they hated Shillery even more or they never vote Democrat. That leaves maybe fifteen percent who really like the guy."

"Minority rules! It's scary."

"Yeah. When little people cast big shadows, the sun is about to set."

"What do you think could happen next?"

"As this creaky journalist sees it?"

"Yes."

"I think Cain's biggest problems won't be domestic but global. He might get away with pushing people around in this country, but foreign leaders won't put up with his crap. They'll say we can sell our resources and buy our products from China and India and dozens of other countries, and instead of foreign nations forming alliances with us they'll form alliances against us. You know how long it took for Rome to fall, from pinnacle to pit?"

"How long?"

"Eight years. Template that timeframe onto 2017–2025."

"Can't we do anything between now and then?"

"I don't know. But I have an idea."

I Hear It in my Deep Heart's Core

NEXT MORNING, Hod parks in front of a brick bungalow with white trim and a narrow porch across its front. Cane in hand, he limps onto the driveway along the dwelling's side to the back corner. Turns and steps across a patch of lawn to a door nearly hidden in a tangle of vines sprawling over the back of the house. His right hand propped on his cane, his left hand lifts to the door…

nuk nuk

A long minute later the door slits open an inch. Appears a suspicious eye in an elderly face. The eye brightens, the door widens. The same little man in the same rumpled red and black flannel shirt. "Hi Hod," his tenor words crisp and quick, "Had an idea I'd see you soon."

"I can't believe he won!" Hod says as he steps inside.

"Me either. Shillery would have been a dunce but Cain is dangerous. The Lyin' King! While claiming to uphold democracy that moral dwarf kindles its destruction, and his running mate is no better. Rufus Shilling, the mesmerizing televangelist from Montana. 'The consummate communicator,' the media calls him. With his clarion voice and fiery red hair and long arms waving above his lanky six-and-a-half foot frame, he may strike a charismatic pose, but his morals have more skin than marrow."

"What on earth makes a person like Cain tick?"

"I remember the first thing he said when he announced he would run for president. He impudently said, 'I'm rich,' as if the whole world would want to bow at his feet and look up to him as their leader. I said to myself we won't need to worry about *him* being president. But it never crossed my mind that millions of poor and deprived people would project his success onto themselves and imagine being someone they could never become on their own."

"And he who has them under his spell will exploit them for all they're worth."

"You just spelled the name Cain. If he has his way, you know what he'll do with my beloved abstraction, the American people?"

"I have a mighty good idea. What's yours?"

"He'll turn our poorest citizens into wage slaves who will suffer from vanished opportunities and be chained to penurious jobs when they can find one. Then he'll do the same with the next class above, from the underside upward, until the masses are languishing in poverty as Cain and his ermined cronies feed on their carcasses like vultures on carrion. Cain promises to lower taxes for the middle class? He'll do it —by causing them to lose their jobs."

"He's already committed a few crimes before he's been inaugurated."

"And he's found the perfect place for a criminal on the lam to hide. Remember during his political campaigns he urged his supporters to attack his adversaries?"

"I remember."

"That's yesterday's clue for what tomorrow he'll do. In his oval den he'll exacerbate racial and religious animosities, peddle lies, pit brother against brother and worker against worker, heap one's burning grievances onto another's fiery discontent until every mind smolders with hate and nothing is left but ashes and apathy."

"Where's the love card when we need it?"

"There's no more love in Cain's kind than you'd find milk in a male hyena. When they set a trap for you, loving the trapper only draws you nearer the trap, only gilds the poison lilly. Promises of love make the choicest baits, don't they?"

"Makes you want to hide somewhere."

"Another page in his plan. Fill people with fear, make them forget to be brave. Shrinking violets are easy to pick, aren't they? They look pretty to the picker but to each other they're dead in the water. But when everyone is so weak he can easily control them you know what he'll do?"

"What's that?"

"He'll weave a massive loom of propaganda —for make no mistake, Cain is a ruthless propagandical animal. He'll begin with a frame a nation wide, whose warp and weft will include millions of loose threads, and he'll look for fibers that are raw and tough and have a primitive grain, then he'll immerse them in a large melting pot filled with ignorance and hatred, and cover them and allow to simmer. When each thread is limp enough to manipulate yet strong enough to retain its shape, he'll weave them into warps of passion and wefts of prejudice until the fabric will resist rough handling and won't unravel, and with the shuttle of coercion he'll add a few more, more, more, ever more. And he'll pattern the threads with colorful slogans that when endlessly repeated will strengthen the weave, and he'll watch for any snags of facts and logic which can unexpectedly appear and must be eliminated lest they weaken the weave. When he's done, the initial loose fibers will be a tight fabric whose colors have such an alluring stench that when covering the length and breadth of the loom can turn millions of maggots into swarming flies."

"Some loom!"

"I unheartily concur. Once he locks everything down until we're living like animals in a cage, if the natives get restless he'll declare martial law. Then to 'restore order' he'll cancel elections, abolish Congress, dismiss judges, banish the media —and if anyone refuses to howl with the pack, grind them up like so much fish feed. The new world disorder!"

"So what can we do?"

"Find clever ways to tell the truth," the little man turns from the door into the shadowy hall behind, looking over his shoulder for Hod to follow. "Ways that are so undeniable and clearly obvious that a person would feel like a fool to deny them. Be truthocrats! Be members of the Above Right! Nudgucate, fudgucate, pitchucate, snitchucate, pushucate, add to the fire of our ire the fuel of truth and morals and logic —and tell it over and over. The harder you hammer the nail of truth the deeper you drive it in!" His slippered feet whisper down the hall, Hod limping a cane-aided step behind. "Then keen your conscience with courage. Courage, that's where victory begins! Sow the seeds of courage in the fertile soil of freedom, and know the more you fight now the less you fight later, even if the red and blue becomes the black and blue." As he reaches the door aglow with light his little face shines like an ember in the dark. "We may face brutality, we may need to overcome trickery, we may even become martyrs —but our efforts will be stenciled on the memories of every citizen, rich and poor, near and far." He steps into his lair of computers old and new, Hod on his shoulder. "It'll take time, but long before each of us is a puppet on a frayed string, Cain will be brought as a sheep before his shearers and he will be damned for his deeds and will make his grave with the wicked." The little man pulls back the armchair in front of his keyboard and sits as Hod leans his shoulder against the wall nearby. "But as we twin our talents we mustn't be hateful, because hate corrodes the soul, and steals the pasture as you buy the horse, and instead of openly condemn him we'll covertly expose him. Let *his* words denounce him as the Devil he is and add feathers to our wings."

"Some people may think we're treasonous."

"Treasonous? Whenever Cain impugns the Constitution he's the treasoner! *He's* the one who profanes it with repression —forcing others into a mold they can't fit into, the essential evil that underlies so many other evils! What underlies denying women their prenatal rights? Repression. What underlies denying Muslims their rights? Repression. What underlies denying Latinos their rights? Repression. End repression! When you feel its hateful weight clamping down on you, revoke it, rescind it, repeal it, repudiate it, eradicate it as if a virulent disease —slay it till it breathes no more!"

"Thou shalt not repress thy neighbor."

"Hey, that's good! You just make that up?"

"Been carrying it around awhile."

"That's one way to laugh a fact into a serious chat."

"So, you have any ideas how two Davids can fight this Goliath?"

"I'm glad you brought that up. Remember the bug I made for the debates last winter?"

"How could I forget it?"

"It would be nice if we could tape his private conversations and send the transcripts to a newspaper, don't you think?"

"With forty years of journalism under my belt I don't need to think a second about that. But how can we tape his private conversations if we can't get into his big white house?"

"Let's see. Since a TV network won't be broadcasting them, we wouldn't be able to send our ghost friend upstream on its broadband frequency, but we wouldn't want to if a nationwide audience isn't watching. But we could make something that would detect a reference circuit from, say, up to a half mile away. But it would require a strong antenna. Something long and narrow."

"What will I do, walk around with a pair of rabbit ears on my head?"

"No. But you could walk with one between your hand and your feet."

A crafty smile spreads over Hod's face. "And," looking around at the electronics walling the room, "where might I find one of those?"

"I thought you would ask," the little man smiles. He smoothes the front of his red and black flannel shirt and kneels under the counter between the keyboard and his chair. A moment later rises holding a bronze anodized aluminum cane with a T-shaped handle.

"I'll be damned," Hod grins.

"It's made of a durable alloy that's strong and stable and has a sturdy underpinning."

"Ha haa, that's important for everyday use."

"It also has a carrying capacity of 250 pounds and the factory offers custom sizing at no extra cost." He admires the anodized cane as if it's a work of art. "Fashionable, wouldn't you say?"

"Why don't you make me a dozen and a cane stand to boot."

"Oooh, let's see how this one works first."

Hod grasps the cane. "Kinda heavy in the shaft. What's in it?"

"It contains a conical receptor with a high-gain amplifier."

"How would it know the voice is him?"

"Voice recognition software. That technology's been around awhile. If you're within a half mile of that bantamweight statesman you can detect his voice. Simply remove the rubber cap from the bottom of the cane and rotate its tip in a megaphone-like arc, and when it detects the voice it's programmed to hear, first you'll hear it faintly, then you wave the tip a little up and down and side to side, until the voice is loud and clear. Once you've slaved the voice, you can listen to his statecraft and any voice nearby he's talking to. You'll be the proverbial four hundred-pound hacker who lives in Jersey."

"Why's the handle T-shaped instead of round?"

The little man takes the cane and holding up the T-shaped handle removes a rubber cap from one end. On its face, two prongs like the prongs on the end of an extension cord.

"How does it work?"

"You plug an extension cord into a nearby outlet and," pointing to the end of the handle, "plug the other end here."

Hod smiles. "How can I transcribe what I hear? My shorthand isn't that good anymore."

The little man removes the cap from the T handle's other end. On its face, two slots like the slots in an electric outlet. "You plug a tape recorder into here, then you can record what the antenna detects. With the recorder's volume control you can lower his voice if he talks too loud."

"I bet I'll do a lot of that. So, where I can buy a tape recorder that'll work with this?"

"No buying necessary," the little man turns in his chair and points to a pocket-size tape recorder tucked in a far corner by the Apple Newton. "Why don't you exercise your bad knees and get that for me."

Hod limps over and lifts it and a cord dangling from it.

The little man plugs the cord into the end of the T handle. "There you go. It works like one of those broadcast vans you see parked outside a stadium during a sporting event. In fact, to get results as good as a broadcast van you may need a technical director, a producer, an editor, an audio mixer, a graphic artist, plus an instant replay coordinator in case something exciting happens, and a color balancer to make sure what appears on a TV display looks nice for the folks back home. Think you can handle all that?"

"If my head can't my knees can," Hod grins. "Anything else I'll need?"

"Come to think of it, you'll need a way to mount this antenna on a mobile tower that can move in any direction and contains a memory device that can find windows indoors, because the amplifier receives signals more clearly through a pane of glass than a solid wall."

"Would it help if this tower has bad knees?"

The little man nods. "If any security spooks see you, I doubt they'd suspect an old man who needs a cane to get around. The harder you lean on it, the more camouflaged you'll be."

"So, it would help if my knees ached like hell when I was using this."

"If I were you, I'd flaunt my disability as strenuously as I could."

"That's a big change! Maybe I should carry two of these instead of one."

"One will do for now. You still have some friends over at *The Post?*"

"Got a flock of em. I gave them so much business for forty years they ought to build a monument of me out front."

"Maybe they will after this is over. All you need is a place within a half mile of the Boss's happy home and you can transcribe his statecraft whenever you want."

"Maybe overlooking Lafayette Square, with his big white house staring at me from the other side. With all the people I used to know in that town, I should be able to find a cubbyhole somewhere with a window facing his desk. Same with Capital Hill. It has plenty of places if he says anything important there. But how will I know when and where he'll have a meeting?"

"His press secretary usually keeps his schedule in his laptop, and I can hack into that, a high school cybersleuth can do the same, and from the internet we can get plans of his house."

"Looks like I'll be well equipped and well informed."

"With some photos of his office and his cronies, you could spruce up a transcript with a few scenic details that would make your leak seem like it came from someone near his desk instead of hundreds of feet outside."

"I'll make my prose as purple as ripe plums."

"But if you hear anyone tearing up his office like they're searching for a plant, turn this off for a while so your receptor won't be detected. And if any spook stops you, act like an old man hobbling on a cane."

Hod holds the cane in his hands. Admires it from its handle to the tip of its shaft. Lifts it like it's a rifle and fits its T-shaped handle into his shoulder and aims its tip at a monitor mounted on the wall like he's a sniper. "Ha haa," he lustily laughs, "I'll make deep throat sound like a deaf mute."

"Your knees will certainly enjoy the rest."

"I feel a big mission falling on our small shoulders," lowering the cane.

"From our few loaves of bread we'll feed the five thousand. It shouldn't be hard, since your target is large, loud, and hollow."

"Maybe it's leaking in a few places."

"You'd be the best to find them."

"I'll just be an old retired journalist, harmless as an ant, who's only reporting what's best for the U S of A. I sure won't fit any social profile most security officers might look for."

"I'd hate to be a peach-fuzzed cybersleuth anywhere nearby when you're hard at work. They might round them all up and waterboard them till they 'confessed', then send them to Guantanamo for a long vacation in the tropics. So, how far is it from here to there?"

"Ooh, hundred and twenty miles. Easy morning or afternoon ride."

"Too bad Tom Jefferson isn't still around. He'd love to come along for the ride."

"So would his buddy James over on the next hill. Madison lived nearby too. What a carload of company they would make!"

"If you know your American history so well, in the painting *Washington Crossing the Delaware*, which James is holding the American flag?"

"Madison?"

"Nope, Monroe."

OVERHEARD IN THE OVAL OFFICE

F ACING THE PANE overlooking Lafayette Square, Hod aims the cane at the White House beyond. Waves its tip up down right left…

"…Hey Boss, the Feds are gonna investigate us."

"What do you mean us? When it comes to this shit, you don't know me and I don't know you."

"But they have ways of finding what they're looking for. Documents, taped phone calls, confessions, you know how they work."

"I know how we work too. We'll conceal or destroy every record of what we did. Go through every pocket of every suit you wore over there, go through every bag you carried, your billfold, your computer, every electronic device."

"What if anyone in the media asks us about this?"

"Say nothing. Stonewall the hell out of this, Disappear somehow. If you can't avoid em, say the sore-loser Democrats cooked this up to undermine the legitimacy of my presidency, say I'm better than crooked Shillery would've ever been with all her lies, say anything about Russia is all lies, fake news."

"But they're tricky, Boss, and they don't give up."

"I know one way to make them give up. Fire them. If they get a little close I'll fire their asses, big tool in the box. But we can put our own public face on this. Paint the F.B.I. as snoopers in cahoots with Obama's crowd who caved to the hateful media's lies. The media can tell the truth only one way but they can tell a lie twenty ways, which way will keep their jobs longer? We can undermine them as well as they can undermine us."

Minutes pass…

"Anything else, Boss?"

"We'll rally our political allies to rebut them. Cabinet. Congressors. Senators. Judges —no, maybe not judges, least for now. We got lots of candy we can feed those who are willing to see things our way……"

FROM *THE WASHINGTON POST*:
F.B.I. INVESTIGATES CAIN'S TIES WITH RUSSIA

WASHINGTON — The F.B.I. is investigating the possibility that President Cain and his campaign staff conspired with Russia to influence the 2016 election. Its Director, Clarian E. Valley said, "The likelihood that Russia may have interfered in our recent presidential election is vitally important to our nation's future, because if we can't hold an honest election without it being influenced by a foreign country, we are vulnerable to vitiation and eventual destruction. However," Mr. Valley added, "this investigation is primarily concerned with whether Russia may have interfered with the election, not whether its interference may have altered the election's outcome."

American intelligence agencies already have evidence that Vladimir Putin of Russia directed a covert effort to damage Shillery Mitten's chances of winning the election and aid Conan Cain. These efforts included hacking the Democratic National Committee and releasing embarrassing emails through the website WikiLeaks, during which some of Cain's associates reportedly were in repeated contact with Russian officials. Last July when WikiLeaks began releasing the hacked emails, Morton Eele, a foreign policy adviser to Cain, visited Moscow for a speaking engagement but has declined to say who he met there. The FBI has obtained a warrant to monitor Eele on suspicions that he knowingly engaged in clandestine intelligence activities with Moscow. This warrant presents the strongest evidence to date that the FBI believes a minion of Cain may have contacted Moscow and met with foreign operatives during Cain's presidential campaign for reasons related to his being elected.

Two mornings ago Cain posted a number of Twitters denying any collusion with Russia and harshly criticizing the investigation's leaks of classified information. But later, in a meeting in the assumed privacy of the Oval Office, Cain and several people who had assisted in his presidential campaign did anything but deny any collusion with Russia to influence the 2016 election. Trusting each other in a we're-in-this-together atmosphere oiled with glasses of fine wine and trays of knishes topped with creme fraiche and caviar, this cabal gaily mapped a strategy for dealing with this crisis.

Cain said they should "conceal or destroy every record of what we did," and if they can't avoid the media, "Say the sore-loser Democrats cooked this up to undermine the legitimacy of my presidency, say I'm better than crooked Shillery would've ever been with all her lies, say Russia is all lies, fake news." He added, "We'll put our own public face on this. We'll paint the F.B.I. as snoopers in cahoots with Obama's crowd who caved to the hateful media's lies. We'll say the media can tell the truth only one way but they can tell a lie twenty ways, which way will keep their jobs longer? We can undermine them as well as they can undermine us." He concluded by saying, "We'll rally our political allies to rebut them. Cabinet. Congressors. Senators. We got lots of candy we can feed those who are willing to see things our way."

Despite F.B.I. Director Valley emphasizing that the investigation isn't concerned whether Russia's possible interference altered the election's outcome, California Senator Dina Finestone said that Russian interference in our presidential election "reversed the result," adding that briefings by our government have so far revealed a "very sophisticated effort" by Moscow to derail

Shillery Mitten's campaign. "I have been astonished at what was a two-year effort by Russia to spearfish, to hack, to provide misinformation and propaganda when and where it could. As for President Cain, this is a fearfully divided nation right now, and he is doing nothing to bring it together."

From every direction it seems, leaks, hints, innuendos, and other percolations from private meetings and secret parlors in and around Washington regarding Cain's possible collusion with Russia continue to pour holy oil on the fires of indignation smoldering in the minds of many Americans.

FROM *THE WASHINGTON POST:*
MEXICO WON'T PAY FOR CAIN'S WALL

WASHINGTON— President Conan Cain may have plans to build a 2,000 mile (3,200 km) wall between the United States and Mexico to keep illegal migrants from entering our country, but two days ago in an Oval Office conversation with Mexican President Enrique Pêa Nieto, Nieto said repeatedly that Mexico won't pay a peso for such a barrier despite, as he said to Cain, "your public claims to the contrary."

During this conversation which Cain and at least two advisors listened to beside a speaker phone on his desk, President Nieto said, "It is evident that we have some differences with this policy of the new government of the United States concerning the topic of the wall, that I have said time and again Mexico will not pay." He further asserted that, "It is not our wall...Our government had nothing to do with originating this idea...If any part is ever built it will not be on our side of the border between our nations...No one in my administration needs to familiarize themselves with any part of its plans."

"Furthermore," Nieto added, "many of the aliens that Americans have apprehended after entering their country are not Mexicans but come from Pan-American nations further south, and our nation has in no way encouraged or assisted any of them from coming from their country through ours to yours." He also said that "Mexico doesn't believe in walls," but that despite his differences with America's President, "Our country offers its friendship to the American people." At all times Pẽa Nieto's voice was cordial, even congenial, and, not to anyone's surprise, he spoke English more fluently than did Cain.

President Nieto's comments contrasted with President Cain's, who after the phone call insisted with his advisors that Mexico will pay to build a barrier along its American border. "We're going to build a wall. It will happen. Remember this, okay?" Cain even insulted his own citizens by saying, "If we can't make Mexico pay for it, we'll make Americans pay for it. We'll say they're paying to keep those wetbacks from stealing their jobs," adding, "We'll blame this on Obama since he let millions of illegal immigrants enter this country the last eight years."

However, this crisis has existed along America's southern border for many years before Obama entered office. Congress must also approve funding to build Cain's wall, estimated to cost ten billion dollars.

The next day in a nationally televised speech, former Mexican President Felipe Calderon said that, "President Cain may want to build a wall across our mutual border to keep illegal migrants out, but don't expect Mexico to pay for it," and he called Cain a "not very well-informed man."

A more portentous aspect of this crisis was voiced by Mexican senator Armando Rios Piter, who heads a committee on foreign relations in his country, who says that this week he will introduce a bill that Mexico will buy corn from Brazil and Argentina instead of the United States. He added, "It is a good way to tell them that this hostile ambition has consequences." Ormond Clinche, a senior analyst at DTN, an agricultural management firm, also said, "If Mexico starts buying corn from other countries, it will affect America's corn market and ripple through our agricultural economy and beyond."

This consequence could well hit our country where it hurts. America is the world's largest exporter of corn and Mexico is one of our biggest buyers. Much of our corn goes into their food, from tacos sold by vendors on city streets to dishes served in fine restaurants. Also since NAFTA became law in 1994, American corn shipments to Mexico have skyrocketed from $391 million in 1995 to $2.4 billion in 2015, the most recent year of available data.

In that great gossip column known as the globe, especially in over-the-fence conversations with close neighbors, ignoring these economics doesn't augur well for the instigator of such inhospitality. Fiscally these opportunities are kin to cash crops ready to harvest; and instead of planting seeds for further growth, both agriculturally and diplomatically, President Cain would pull these potential windfalls by their roots and trample them under his feet. If he continues to foment such ill will with our international neighbors, fulfilling his slogan, Make America Great Again, may well be a labor that falls on the shoulders of America's next president.

FROM THE PRESIDENT'S NEWS CONFERENCE

I AM HERE TODAY to update the American people on the incredible progress that has been made in the last two months since my inauguration." The President, a shingle of blond hair combed over his forehead like the eave of a roof, assumed an imperious air, now and then raising his little right hand and making a little O with his elfin thumb and forefinger. "We have made incredible progress. I don't think there's ever been a president elected who in this short time has done what we've done. The stock market has hit record numbers, as you know. And there has been a tremendous surge of optimism in the business world. Very different.

"I'm giving this news conference directly to the American people, with the media present, because much of the media doesn't get it. They actually get it, but they don't write it. Let's put it this way. Much of the media in Washington, D.C., along with New York, Los Angeles in particular, speaks not for the people, but for the special interests and for those profiting off a very, very obviously broken system. The press has become so dishonest that if we don't talk about it, we are doing a tremendous disservice to the American people. Tremendous disservice. We have to talk to find out what's going on, because the press honestly is out of control. The level of dishonesty is out of control. This administration is running like a fine-tuned machine, yet I turn on the TV, open the newspapers and I see stories of lies and chaos. Chaos.

"I'll give you an example from *The Washington Post*, front page, big massive story, that was more disgraceful than any story the failing *New York Times* has said, that said the morning after I was inaugurated I telephoned David Duke. I never talked to David Duke in my life. Never, not once, complete lie. The story also said I called some people in this country a nasty word, people in this country who the previous administration left behind, some of the most wonderful people in this country, who have supported me from the beginning, that I have tremendous respect for, said I called them mutts. I never said such a thing. Such nasty lies, the exact opposite of the truth, totally made up. They totally misrepresented the truth, I have to tell you, totally misrepresented. I can't believe the hatred, the lies. I said give us the retraction. They never gave us a retraction...

"I'll give you another example. I called, as you know, Mexico. It was a very, very confidential, classified call. And in calling Mexico, I figured, oh, well that's, I spoke to the president of Mexico, I had a good call, we talked about some confidential things. All of a sudden, people are finding exactly what we said, it's out there for the world to see. It's supposed to be confidential or classified. And I'm saying, the first thing I thought of when I heard about it is: How does the press get this information that's classified? How do they do it? Not only that, the story changed some things I said from truths to lies. Actual lies. One lie said if I can't make Mexico pay for the wall I'll make Americans pay for it, I'll say they're paying to keep Mexicans from stealing their jobs. I never said that. Never said anything like that. All nasty lies, all fake news.

"You know what it is? Here's the thing." Up goes the little 0 again formed by his elfin fingers. "I don't mind bad stories. I can handle a bad story better than anybody as long as it's true and I'm okay with that. But I'm not okay when it is fake. The public isn't, you know, they read newspapers, they see television, they watch. They don't know if it's true or false because they're not involved. I'm involved. So I know when the media is telling the truth or when it's not. I just see many, many untruthful things. I know when I should get good and when I should get bad. And sometimes I'll say, "Wow, that's going to be a great story." And I'll get killed. And the press should be ashamed. Really ashamed..."

QUESTION FROM THE PRESS... "*The Washington Post* recently reported that F.B.I. Director Clarion Valley is currently investigating if you conspired with Russia to influence the 2016 election. In a meeting in the Oval Office with several people who assisted in your campaign, it was reported that you and they, and I quote from the article in *The Post*, 'Decided to conceal or destroy everything we did,' and we should, 'Say the sore-loser Democrats cooked up the investigation to undermine the legitimacy of my presidency, say I'm better than crooked Shillery would've ever been with all her lies.' Also in this meeting you reportedly said the F.B.I. is a 'A crew of snoopers in cahoots with Obama's crowd who caved to the hateful media's lies;' that 'The media can tell the truth only one way but they can tell a lie twenty ways, which way will keep their jobs longer;' and 'We can undermine them as well as they can undermine us.' How true are these allegations?"

"I can tell you, speaking for myself, I own nothing in Russia. I have no loans in Russia, I don't have any deals in Russia. Russia is fake news, all lies put out by the media."

Hod Hawksbill leans back in his chair in front of the TV he is watching, muttering, "He ducked the question, which was did he conspire with Russia to influence the 2016 election? If he doesn't answer a question, imagine he answers it in a way that hurts him the most —that's the code— then ask my trusted contacts what they think? Amazing the leaks that spring this way! He says he owns nothing in Russia, has no loans in Russia, has no deals in Russia? When he speaks surface truths like this it means he's doing something deeper that's worse —that's the code. So don't waste your time nosing for ownings or loans or deals, listen for leaks in dark places, drip, drip, drip."

"…The real news," Cain continues, "is Obama's people probably made it up, because they're there, they were there at the time. And, you know, you can talk all you want about Russia, which was all, you know, fake news, a fabricated deal, to try and make up for the loss of the poor loser Democrats and the press plays right into it. I know a couple of the people the media claims were involved in all this, and they know nothing about it, they weren't in Russia, never made a phone call to Russia, never received a phone call, all lies, all fake news…"

Hod mumbles, "He thinks that when he lies the public will believe him.

'His people know nothing about it?' They know *everything* about it. 'They weren't in Russia?' They *were* in Russia. 'Never made a phone call.' They made *several* phone calls. Reverse suppositions —if you know the code you know the road. Leaks, here I come. May my bucket runneth over!"

"... And," Cain continued, "I'll tell you what else I see. I see tone. The tone is such hatred. You have to admit that. I know what's good and bad. And when they change it and make it sound really bad, sometimes something that should be very positive, they'll make it negative. I don't even know where they got some of those stories in the first place. They're put out by people in the news agencies or so-called anonymous sources, every one is a criminal leak, a criminal lie. In all my life I've never seen more dishonest media. We got to stop it. And we're looking at them very —very, very serious. I've gone to all of the people in charge of the various agencies and we're, I've actually called the Justice Department, one thing I felt it was very important, to look into the leaks. I mean they are absolute lies, and the news is fake, so much is fake. I think you'll see it stopping because since I became President we have our new people going in place, and I hope we can correct it ...."

In an analysis of the President's press conference, one of America's foremost news anchors, Edwin Burrow, said: "In a monotonously prolonged display of angst by a head of state, President Cain, instead of using this conference to inform the public of matters of serious concern, did much to amputate himself from those who could more widely inform the public of these concerns as well as promote the amity he seeks. Indeed, the President acted less like a statesman talking intelligently about important issues than an emotionally incontinent person who can't control his baser thoughts. As such, his complaints aren't so much the media bearing the news as the news the media bears, that rather than suffering from the opprobrium of a hateful press he is suffering from the chafings of chronic corruption. Well should the media's tarring his hide with a moral brush make his skin crawl at premonitions that his brayings would alienate the public."

WHO GAINS MOST IN CAIN'S TAX OVERHAUL?

WASHINGTON — As President Conan Cain turns his attention to overhauling America's tax code, Americans everywhere are wondering who will reap the biggest benefits on tax day?

Will it be home builders?

Or retailers?

Or charities?

Or the elderly?

Guess again: President Cain and his wealthiest confreres. In a proposal that could make America's frailest shoulders carry the greatest burden, if Cain and his cronies get their way the revised tax code will be a portfolio of candy opportunities that will fatten their fortunes for years to come while the take-home pay of most middle-class Americans will decrease. As the flame of greed burned brightly in their breasts, with compound interest these acolytes knelt at the altar of avarice —the Oval Office— in hopes that by revising the tax code to their advantage they could obtain the following perks and pork…

☞ Real estate developers would be able to use large amounts of tax-deductible debt to finance land deals. One crony joked to Cain, "You'll be the king of debt for life."

☞ High-income profits would enjoy lower tax rates. This munificently pleased his profiteering pals. One quipped, "It is nice that our President is so sensitive to those issues that mean the most to us."

☞ The corporate income tax rate would be sharply reduced from 35 percent to 21 percent. One of this cluster of monetary muscle said, "These reductions would significantly increase the donations we make to our favorite charities: ourselves."

☞ Create a "tax holiday" (the length of time to be determined later) that would enable individuals and companies having stockpiled cash offshore to repatriate these funds at a reduced tax rate.

☞ The alternate minimum tax rate would be eliminated, which in 2005 alone cost Cain $31,000,000.

☞ Eliminate tax benefits for college students. Interest paid on student loans would no longer be tax deductible, nor would tuitions reduced by students working as researchers and teaching assistants. While Secretary of Education Gretchen Verbose discussed this with President Cain she said, "Less then four percent of Americans with doctorate degrees today identify as Republicans."

Replied Cain, "We don't want to educate people like that. The less educated they are, the more ignorant they are, the poorer they are. The more we can keep em poor the more we can manipulate em, get em to vote for us. If they're uneducated, why change em?"

Like Islamic extremists, Cain and his cronies know an educated person is more an enemy than a friend.

If Cain gets his way, he'll be a peddlar of prosperity for the few at the top of the economic food chain while being a peddlar of poverty for the many at the bottom. Representative Herman Horne of New York said, "Any tax code revisions should be delayed until Congress can review Mr. Cain's tax returns to see if his planned revisions would personally benefit him."

Concerning Cain's proposed tax reforms for college students, Helena Greenway, President of the American Council on Education, said, "Cain's tax code would worsen the student debt crisis, force many students out of school, and discourage many others from entering masters and doctorate programs. Branches can't grow without roots; and by lessening opportunities for our finest students to earn advanced degrees, Cain is cutting the roots from which spread the fruiting branches of our nation's enduring prosperity."

A noted authority on tax law, Lionel Dalance, CEO of MRT Advisers in New York, weighed in by saying, "You would need a 6 percent GDP growth rate to make Cain's revised tax code work, and I don't see it. It is more likely that his plan will create an enormous shortfall in tax revenue, which would lead most Americans to become heavily mortgaged by a soaring national debt. Also if the President is dishonest, more taxpayers will believe they too can be dishonest. Since the IRS can audit only a small percent of the nation's tax returns, this loss alone could cost the nation billions of dollars."

If Cain by revising the tax code creates an "Age of Chiselry" for him and his acquisitive cronies, every dollar Cain gains would be a dollar lost by the citizens he represents. Talk about taxation without representation! But getting a Congress dominated by Republicans, many who also wallow in the tallow of fat portfolios, to vote down these revisions may be an empty dream.

FROM *THE WASHINGTON POST:*
CAIN'S FINGERS IN THE AMERICAN PIE

WASHINGTON — The Mother of our Laws, the American Constitution, states in Article 1, Section 9, popularly known as the Emoluments Clause: "No Person holding any Office of profit or trust under them shall without the Consent of the Congress accept any present, emolument, office, or title, of any kind whatever, from any king, prince, or foreign state."

Yet yesterday in the assumed privacy of the Oval Office, while sipping glasses of 1999 Montrachet Grand Cru Chardonnay (reportedly costing $1,250 per bottle) and munching blinis slathered with Russian caviar, in a classic example of the father shaking the tree while the children gather the apples, President Cain and his two oldest sons, Adam and Conan Jr., and his older daughter Connie and her husband Neville Nisalt, gaily discussed how they could leverage the father's public office for private gain, the chief beneficiary being the Cain Corporation which umbrellas over a hundred family businesses worldwide. Here are some of the ways this clan discussed how they could use the Presidency to stuff their pockets at the expense of American taxpayers ...

☞ How to build a hotel in Argentina and license its operation to a third party who would pay Cain Corp annual fees for the right to use the Cain brand. Though the family wouldn't profit directly from this venture, the more successful it is the more valuable the business would be after the President left office. They gaily discussed how they could offer

WHEN LITTLE MEN
CAST BIG SHADOWS...

THE SUN IS ABOUT TO SET

local government officials diplomatic positions, salaries for nonexisting jobs, kickbacks, and free rooms if they would approve building codes and other regulations that normally would stall the project. These unethical practices would violate the Foreign Corrupt Practices Act (FCPA) which forbids American companies from participating even unknowingly in bribery schemes in foreign countries.

☞ How to revive a long-stalled hotel project in Azerbaijan, one of the most corrupt countries in the world. Though Cain claims he has placed the project in control of his children and won't discuss it with them, here he openly discussed how his daughter, who manages the project, would work with local authorities to develop it. During this discussion he joked that before his inauguration he pledged "his company would not pursue any new deals in foreign countries" — meaning he would eagerly revive old ones. Merely by associating with such corruption, Cain violates the FCPA.

☞ How to profit from their relation with Ms. Qi-Ting Huan, director of Global Alliance Associates, a consulting firm that helps American corporations, the U.S. Department of Commerce, and the U.S. Trade & Development Agency "develop strategic relationships with prominent decision-makers in China" —i.e. curry favor with the Chinese government. To facilitate these affiliations Ms. Huan purchased a $16 million penthouse in Cain Corp's 58-story headquarters in New York. Her tenancy would steer an estimated million dollars annually into Cain's coffers from the conferences and other profitable bookings associated with her business activities to be held in the building.

☞ How to renew developing a resort in the Dominican Republic that in 2007 Cain Corp contracted to develop there. Due to a series of financial crises, disagreements, and building code violations this project has since stalled; which now as President he intends to revive. Shortly after his inauguration his son Adam, who has led this project since its inception, publicized Cain's presidency in its promotion literature, and in the Dominican Republic on the proposed site he staged a photo-op with the resort's developers and discussed how to develop the property and pursue related business ventures in this country.

☞ How to use their newly opened Cain International Hotel in Vancouver to advance the family's business interests in the Pacific, particularly Indonesia. Cain's family discussed how to use his Presidency to encourage loyal government leaders and wealthy business people to hold conventions, host promotional events, and book rooms in the hotel —and more ominously, how to withhold or retract such favors from anyone who would disagree with a presidential policy or decision.

☞ How to secretly buy a large tract of land anywhere in the world, design a hotel in its center which, combined with promoting the company brand and converting the raw land to commercial property, would skyrocket the value of the peripheral acreage. The father gaily described how in 1982 he purchased 90 acres in Florida for 230,000 dollars, built a hotel on 23 acres in the center, then sold the peripheral acreage to other commercial interests for 5.1 million dollars.

☞ How through a bank in the Netherlands where for years Cain has laundered the dirty money of a number of wealthy Russians, they could clean huge sums of money plundered by patronizing business persons and government decision-makers around the world. The fees for this service would range from 20 to 35 percent depending on what extent, they joked, a customer would want one's "lettuce triple-washed" or "its stains expertly removed." Father Cain said, "For every four or five billion dollars we dry-clean, we make one."

☞ How Cain's children can promote their company's brand and manage their many business holdings worldwide while flying ultra class (i.e. enjoying bed, bath, and breakfast service at 40,000 feet) and being protected by their secret service units at "taxpayers' treat".

Given Cain's proclivity to subordinate public need to private greed, one can only cower at the huge profits his family will likely accrue from such pay-to-play corruptions in their businesses around the world —that every dollar of profit gained by them would be a dollar lost to the taxpaying public, that every job created by these foreign businesses would be a job potentially denied American workers, that every capital gain from eventually selling a business at a profit should be deposited in the United States Treasury. Cain once Twittered this issue by saying "only the crooked media makes this a big deal!" As one can plainly see, the only big deals made here end up in the crooked pockets of our Commander-in-Thief. Indeed greed has mutinied his judgment, and the nation's ship of state is now manned by a family band of pirates. Why can't even billions of dollars still the teeth that gnash at his soul?

FROM *THE WASHINGTON POST:*
JUSTICE DEPARTMENT PROBES CAIN'S FINANCES

RUMORS ARE BECOMING TOO RIFE for the U.S. Department of Justice to ignore the possibility that Conan Cain may be using the office of the Presidency to fill his pockets with profits from his constellation of business activities around the world. As such these distant flyspecks have become motes in the eyes of one of America's most honorable servants of justice, Deputy Attorney General Sansome Driver, who yesterday was appointed to direct an investigation into Cain's personal finances. "Certainly no president has ever had the number of major business activities worldwide as does President Cain, and we understand it may be impossible and even unfair to expect him to cut all his ties with them while he is in office.

"However," Driver emphasized, "in our investigation it is not coin that will judge our conclusions but the conscience behind the flow of currency. As such we have an obligation to the American people to determine if the President is using his office as presses for printing money for himself and his children as well as any of his friends or political connections. We want to be sure that when he makes a dollar in this manner, that dollar is deposited not in his pockets but in the pockets of We the People of the United States.

"At first glance," Driver continued, "this investigation may seem to be nearly impossible to undertake. But as every corporate manager knows, we can examine any business spreadsheet and trace every profit and see that each has a clear direction and a defined limit." Asked if some of Cain's transactions might be so hidden they couldn't be discovered, Driver replied, "Some may well be so, but as we examine his business activities, all we'll be looking for is where that green stuff called dollars came from and where it went.

"For example, if he paints one of his hotels, we don't need to know how many cans of paint he bought and what each cost and what he paid the painters, we can have a professional estimator look at photos of the building and determine these costs, the same as a painter would estimate such work before undertaking it by looking at the building's plans. If Cain doesn't agree with our numbers, it will be up to him to prove they are otherwise. Once we know the hand of transaction, it is easy to find whether the mind behind was thinking of charity or avarice."

If President Cain is planting any seeds of lawless greed in foreign soils richly manured with corruption and shaded from the light of justice, hopefully the Justice Department's investigation will un-

A good name is rather to be chosen than great riches

cover them before their ill-harvested fruits would nourish a despot within our nation's doors.

OVERHEARD IN THE OVAL OFFICE

CANDICE ... CANDICE CURTISS, my Assistant Counselor. Good morning.

"Good morning to you, Boss."

"Got some business we need to go through. Pull up a chair. Okay. Before we get into this, I want to thank you for your lovely appearance on Fox News last Saturday. The way you looked, what you said was impressive, beautiful. You and that host make a nice pair."

"Why thank you. You and I make a nice pair with the work we do here. Like the old song says, I'll do anything for you, dear."

"You don't say ..."

"I just did say it. I'm not going to take it back."

"Nice, the way your hair curls above your shoulders. You brush it often?"

"Few times a day."

"Beautiful. You keep a brush on your desk?"

"In a drawer."

"Good place to keep a brush. You could see this better if you sat over here instead of across the desk." (Sound of a chair moving). "Come closer so you can see both pages. Beautiful."

"So what's on your mind?"

"You look nice this morning. I always like blondes."

"Why, thank you."

"A dollar for your thoughts."

"I was thinking that our lips have known each other for quite some time, but they haven't been improperly introduced."

"Ha, I like that!"

"We can be delicately improper, in case someone is watching."

"Like who?"

"Your wife."

"She's a million miles away in New York. Your husband?"

"He's vanished off the face of the earth somewhere."

"Babe, I think you're really hot."

"Why thank you. I love your hair. It would look nicer though if it was smoother."

"Go ahead…better than a brush."

"There. You look lovely."

"Talk about lovely, that's a lovely dress you're wearing. It's a little distracting though. Why don't you take it off?"

"Here?"

"The carpet's plush."

"Don't you think Lincoln's bed would be a little cozier?"

"Yes, beautiful." (Sound of chairs moving).

"Our arms have known each other for while too, but they haven't been improperly introduced either."

"…Ooh, babe, you're really hot."

Hod waves the cane at the window. "They're moving out of range. " He waves its tip up down right left. *Where's that floorplan?*

"…His bed is so big."

"Every inch is for you, babe."

"He was tall, wasn't he?"

"Six-four."

"No wonder it's so long and wide."

"Mattress made for two. That dress of yours is looking more distracting every second."

"I could use some help removing it."

"Must be hell slipping it over those curves."

"It's *terribly* difficult. Especially the zipper in back."

"Here… (sound of a zipper). "So slender, babe, you're really hot."

"Yess…let me help you with your jacket."

"Better than wiggling my big arms out of these sleeves. Beautiful."

"Your tie must be strangling you."

"I'm waiting for an angel to unstrangle me."

"Present and accounted for. There."

"Beautiful."

"Your shirt would look nicer if it was on the floor."

"Help me with these buttons. Come in from the side."

"Ooh, darling, your arm's so soft on my shoulders."

"Babe, you're really hot."

"Takes one to know one…must be hard unbuckling this when you can barely see it."

"Not the only thing hard there."

"Your fly. Oh honey, yess, yess…your shoes."

"Go ahead and untie them. Need any help with those heels?"

"I can kick them off, but my nylons are terribly clingy."

"Takes a man's touch."

"You said it, brother. Ooh, your hands are so soft."

"I love your legs, so graceful, beautiful."

"Help me with my panties. Yess…faster, love."

"Oh, babe, babe, you're really hot."

"Ooh, ooh honey. Oh give it to me, give it to me. Yeah. Ooh, oooh —OOH! Oh God, oh God."

"Oh, babe, babe…babe…babe…"

"Oh God, oh God -ooh -oh -OH -OH GOD, oooooh oh -oh, oh, oh God. Ooooh."

"Oh, babe, so lovely, beautiful…"

FROM *THE WASHINGTON POST:*
PRESIDENT'S HOTEL BOMBED IN THE PHILIPPINES

MARAVILOSA COVE, Philippines… Sixty miles east of Manila in the Philippines, in a region spotted with national parks and studded with mountains blanketed with jungle beside a magnificent beach of palest gold curving around the emerald waters of Maravilosa Cove, an hour before dawn Sunday morning a huge explosion leveled one of President Conan Cain's global properties, the Gold Coast Resort, killing hundreds of people.

At this five-star hideaway, acclaimed for its stunning views, endlessly sunny weather, and embracingly warm surf, one could enjoy a panoramic view of the bay from one's king-size bed, relish lavish buffets in its three fine restaurants, and relax on the sun-drenched sand and read a favored book, frolic in the nearby surf, and work on a luscious tan. But in a monstrous flash in the dark of night, this famous twelve-story luxury resort fell to a pile of rubble thirty feet high and three hundred feet long.

The most reliable witness of this predawn disaster was a guest luckily suffering from insomnia who a little after four A.M. decided to take a walk along the beach. He was looking toward the hotel 200 feet away when he saw what appeared to be four quick bright flashes in the windows of the central portion of the second floor followed by an earsplitting BOOOOM —then the lower central part of the hotel burst forward and as the surrounding flood-lights went out the floors above fell with a huge roar and the building's two ends pitched inward upon the collapsed center.

The blast was so strong it threw the guest forty feet into the nearby surf. Thankful for the dive he swiftly swam another hundred feet into the cove. When he finally surfaced and looked back, in the light of a waning half-full moon shining above the sea at his back he saw a huge gray cloud where the hotel had been, the beach cluttered with chunks of concrete, and a blanket of dust settling on the surf. Hearing screams from the rubble, he waded out of the surf and helped several people stagger from the debris.

Before sunrise an hour later the parking lot and the edge of the golf course on the inland side of the hotel were crammed with ambulances, police cars, and rescue vehicles amid swarms of rescue workers searching through the debris for survivors. With the rise of the sun arrived two huge front-end loaders who first cleared the streets around the hotel so rescuers could get through, then the loaders began to delicately lift away parts of the rubble where could be heard cries for help. By midmorning 32 injured victims had been extricated and loaded into waiting ambulances that screamed toward local hospitals. Since the hotel offices were on the central part of the first floor, it was impossible to know the exact number of guests and staff remaining in the rubble. But by midmorning, by counting the online registration bookings, estimating the usual 40 or 50 guests who arrived unannounced, and adding the dozen or so staff members who were in the building, the police estimated that about 380 people were laid in their graves by the blast.

A little after ten o'clock, a forensic engineer skilled in examining building failures arrived to assess the destruction. After surveying the site and reading the reports of the witnesses, his first words after the usual introductory civilities were, "This was the work of professionals. They knew precisely what they were doing." As a herd of reporters gathered around him he removed a set of architectural plans from his truck and opened them on its hood to the second floor of the hotel. As he pointed to four rows of little squares extending across the plan he said, "These are the columns that supported the upper floors. Each row has 13 columns spaced 7.0 meters (22.8 feet) apart. The two outer rows of columns align with the two long east and west facades of the hotel, and the two inner rows align with the walls on each side of the floor's central hall. What interests us most here," pointing at the rows of inner columns, "are the five centermost supports along the beach side of the hall. The perpetrators placed a large bundle of explosives, probably in suitcases carried indoors by so-called guests who made reservations in the rooms beside these columns."

Said a reporter, "The witness on the beach said he thought only four explosions occurred. What makes you think there were five?"

"If only four explosions occurred," the engineer replied, "four unexploded columns would have been on one side of the explosion and five on the other," looking over at the rubble, "then the piles on each side would be different sizes. But," pointing left and right, "you can see that the piles of rubble on each side are roughly symmetrical. This leads to the conclusion that five explosions destroyed the central columns and an equal number of four unexploded columns were on each side. As the ten floors above fell, their impact crushed everything below and the continuously reinforced concrete floors pulled in the floors from each end. Look at the fallen end facades," pointing at them, "see how they lay against the ends of the long pile of rubble instead of having fallen straight down. Obviously," bowing his head in grief, "the perpetrators had studied the building's plans."

Asked another reporter, "How were the explosives detonated?"

"These days, they could have been ignited by a battery-powered laptop computer equipped with a wi-fi system that activated electronic receivers mounted in each bundle of explosives. The computer's operator likely wasn't more than a few dozen yards away, so he may have sacrificed his life in the explosion. We'll look for that as we clear the debris."

Asked another, "How do you know this was done by people and not a vehicle, say a car or a truck or even a plane loaded with explosives?"

"By process of elimination. From the witness's description we know the explosives weren't flown or driven in and they detonated completely inside the building. So by *reductio ad absurdem*, they were planted by human hands."

Diosado Macapal, Minister to the President of the Philippines, speaking from the scene declared the attack to be "a horrible terrorist crime," that "those responsible for this appalling violence must be swiftly brought to justice," and that "our crisis response teams are working closely with all relevant authorities." In Washington, Pentagon spokesman Brigadier General Marshall Macomber said, "we unequivocally condemn this terrorist act of violence."

A little after noon the *Manila Bulletin*, the Philippine's leading newspaper, received a phone call saying that Abu Sayyaf, a Philippine Islamist group that pledges allegiance to ISIS and has a history of committing terrorist acts with improvised explosive devices, claimed responsibility for the attack. The caller called the disaster "A calamity for the infidels," adding, "The Infidel-in-Chief will pay for his hatred of our beloved brothers." These remarks obviously referred to President Cain's incendiary rhetoric toward Muslims and ISIS as well as his once calling the Philippines a terrorist nation. Thus the disaster's perpetrators essentially killed two birds with one stone: they sent a symbolic message of anti-American sentiment to the rest of the world, and they demolished a prominent building belonging to America's hawkish president. This attack also may repel future visitors from other global properties bearing the brand of the "Infidel-in-Chief", and fewer businesses may want the Cain brand to embellish a building they own or work in.

Indeed, one could say President Cain is caught between a bomb and a hard place. U.N. Secretary General Antonio Guterres said, "Although we condemn this attack, it seems to have been made against the business interests of America's President more than his government, and we urge him to show restraint." Angela Merkel, Chancellor of Germany said, "While we lament the loss of life at this resort, it was not a military installation whose destruction reduces our nation's ability to defend itself from foreign invaders, and evidently no military secrets or weaponry were kept at the site." The President of Turkey, Recep Erdogan, said, "The Cain brand is associated with values we don't share and don't want to be associated with." And the Prime Minister of Montenegro, Dusko Markovic, who President Cain unceremoniously shoved aside during a NATO summit meeting of Europe's leaders in Brussels last May, said, "This attack did not occur on the soil of any NATO ally, and no member of NATO should be drawn into a conflict in which the antagonists are enemies of each other and not any of us." Relations between America and NATO has cooled since President Cain has derided the nations of NATO for not contributing more to their mutual defense.

Given Cain's anti-terrorism rhetoric, how may he respond to the destruction of one of his global properties and the killing of hundreds of occupants? Will he place our armed services at risk to protect his properties from similar attacks? He'll doubtlessly want to make them more secure; but many are already guarded by surveillance cameras, private guards, and X-ray detectors, and it would cost millions of dollars to protect them with concrete blast barriers and other military installations. Who would pick up the tab: Cain Corp, foreign governments, U.S. taxpayers? It cost Americans three million dollars to secure just one of Cain's properties, his hotel in midtown Manhattan.

Some federal authorities also believe that when Cain became president, he broke the lease of any obligation our government would have to protect his personal businesses. One agent anonymously said, "Our duty is to provide a 24-hour-a-day, 365-day-a-year protective envelope around the president and his family and any property of his they visit, but we have no obligation to protect a Cain property because it is one of his businesses. As devastating as this tragedy was, this hotel was not a diplomatic post and none of the

President's family was physically threatened. But I'm sure this event will induce the Secret Service and U.S. intelligence agencies to keep closer tabs on Cain's properties as part of America's ongoing global war against terrorism."

As the rest of the world anxiously watches, President Conan Cain will hopefully consider this disaster as the price of doing business more than he would use taxpayers' dollars to retaliate against a hidden enemy in a way that could encourage similar disasters in the future.

FROM *THE WASHINGTON POST:*
MANY DIE IN WEST VIRGINIA MINE DISASTER

MALLARD CREEK, West Virginia...A little after dawn yesterday, three tailing waste dams at the Raven Rock Mine near Shady Spring, West Virginia, burst and a wave of liquid mining waste and abraded earth ranging up to five hundred feet wide and forty feet high roared down the valley below for nearly five miles at speeds up to 60 miles an hour and in ten minutes killed at least 278 people. 32 people are still reported missing.

Each of the three dams at Raven Rock Mine was twenty feet high and retained a several-acre lagoon filled with a blackish slurry that connected like links in a chain on the sloping headwaters of Mallard Creek. After a spring and early summer of above-average rainfall that saturated the area's soils, several inches of heavy rain during the previous weekend so sogged the earthen dam retaining the uppermost lagoon that it burst —then the slurry bursting through the breach scoured away the earth on each aside, all of which spilled into the lagoon below with such force that it swept away the second dam, then a wave of slurry and riven earth from the two upper lagoons tore away the third dam and a roaring wall of debris sluiced down the valley of Mallard Creek. As the pull of gravity relentlessly increased its speed the torrent of debris smashed every house in its path, snapped centuries-old trees like toothpicks, washed away cars and trucks as if they were toys, buried eight miles of roads, wiped out dozens of farms and businesses, and destroyed several communities including a corner of Shady Spring. Only when the debris flow reached the fairly level farmland around where Mallard Creek flows into the Glinche River did it begin to slow. Still, it continued a half mile down the Glinche River until it subsided to a sprawling tongue of sludge and tangled foliage whose tip could be measured with a yardstick.

A hillside resident living two miles below the mine who happened to be watching the sun rise from her terrace several hundred feet above the valley said, "First I heard what sounded like a roaring waterfall somewhere upstream. I looked up the valley, and saw a huge brownish-gray wave flowing downhill like pancake batter onto a griddle. Its front was moving about as fast as a car on a two-lane highway, and its crest passed maybe a hundred yards below my house. Huge rocks were tumbling in the muddy liquid, and trees were sticking out like prickers."

Now as one stands at the site of the three former lagoons and looks down the valley, a scant trace of the three earthen dams remains and the lagoons' basins look slick as the bottom of a bathtub. And the lovely Appalachian valley beyond, whose residents for generations have taken pride in their rugged culture and inspiring history, who live by the Bible and sleep under handmade quilts and dance to lively bluegrass music, who when John Denver sang, "Country roads, take me home, to the place I belong, West Virginia, mountain mama, take me home, country roads," believe he was singing for them —has lost something priceless that would take a lifetime to regain.

The area's environmental damage was especially severe. 150 acres of pristine forest were flattened, a rich diversity of flora and fauna was destroyed, and wildlife habitats and productive farmlands were blanketed with a Noah's flood of toxic silt containing known carcinogens as cadmium and arsenic, harmful metals as mercury and selenium, and dangerous chemicals as sulfuric oxide which in the presence of air and water forms sulfuric acid that combines with trace metals existing in the raw coal to form added toxins. These substances are dangerous to breathe, taint irrigation water, kill fish, pollute ground waters, contaminate local wells and drinking supplies, sicken people, cause pregnant women to miscarry, and create a mother lode of other consequences. Everywhere the valley's woodsy fragrance has been snuffed by a fetid stench, and the continually flowing toxins have already fowled rivers in three states. A popular spring that local residents had drawn water from since the early 1800s which had given the town of Shady Spring its name now lies buried under tons of reeking muck, as is picturesque Howard's Mill, a local attraction whose overshot millwheel and mossy millrace straddled Mallard Creek and had ground corn brought by local farmers since before the Civil War. And the locals no longer say there's good fishing in Mallard Creek.

However, according to many residents here (nearly every person interviewed for this article chose to remain anonymous), all this swiftly wrought devastation began months ago. According to them, the seeds of destruction were planted last February 16 when President Conan Cain stabbed to death with his repealing pen the Stream Protection Rule, an Obama-era regulation that restricted coal companies from carelessly dumping mining waste into streams and waterways. Apparently this repeal also repealed much of many mine owners' consciences concerning that foundation of any community's prosperity, the environment —as since the bill's signing many mines have made less effort to treat their waste and have more openly dumped their residue in the nearest glen or gulch they can find. As for the Raven Rock Mine, since Cain repealed the Stream Protection Rule, production has nearly doubled, and so have the piles of waste accumulating from the mine's operation. Some waste is environmentally benign: dirt used for land reconstruction, vegetation saved for restoring removed ground covers, and rocks crushed into gravel; plus the company runs a small market in lead, cadmium, mercury, and several other metals the bituminous coal contains. But other wastes are highly toxic, particularly those created when the raw coal is refined. At Raven Rock Mine this detritus is ground into dust and treated with chemicals and mixed with volumes of water from Mallard Creek to form a slurrylike tailing that is retained for further treatment in the three lagoons, whose dams must be carefully designed and constructed so they will not fail and afterward must be observingly maintained. Sadly, ignoring this last safeguard spurred the burst of the earthen dams on Mallard Creek.

As one foreman of the mine confidingly explained, in addition to the company's managers allowing a more careless depositing of its tailing waste in the lagoons, they allowed the increased volume of waste to rise to within one foot of the dam's crests instead of a safer and EPA-mandated three feet. "Without a doubt," said the foreman, "the mine's increased production and the EPA looking the other way when the lagoon rose caused the upper dam's sudden failure and the swift failure of the lower two." The foreman said the mine had on its payroll a member of the EPA. "*He's* the one who should have reported the excess rise to the EPA, but he was paid to keep his mouth shut. EPA officials used to be dedicated people who believed their first priority was to balance a business's environmental impact against its economic gain, but Cain ran them off, and under his regime many EPA laws are not being enforced and its present director is corrupt as they come." The foreman seemed to want to get something off his chest as he said, "I consider myself a Conservative Republican. But what Cain is doing is not conservative politics, it's selfish greedy exploitive bullying. His kind have stolen the Conservative name and dirtied it with lowdown greed and self-serving b.s."

Many locals mentioned another failure of the mines: the greedy executives who pocket their profits. One local business owner said, "Before a coal mine opens, it must sign a government contract stating it will remediate any ravaged local environments after the mine closes. But while the mine operates, the executives pay themselves big salaries and don't save a dime for remediation, and to pay the miners they borrow from a bank; and the debts pile up until the company goes under. Last year one coal mine in this state went bankrupt after its president paid himself $30,000,000 in salaries during the ten years the mine operated, then when bankruptcy was eminent he paid him a bonus of $10,000,000. After the company went under, a court found the mine hadn't restored local environments and heavily fined them. But since the mine had no money it paid no fine, plus the miners lost their jobs and health benefits and pensions. That's how you do business in coal mine country."

And who pays? You and me, Mr. and Mrs. Taxpayer. We pay, with our money and our health. And the debts pile up.

An assistant to the mayor of Shady Spring said, "Cain claims he wants to create jobs for the coal miners. But the way he's doing it, for every few miners who find jobs many other workers often lose theirs. Look what happened here," she wiped a tear from her cheek as she looked out her window toward where the debris flow cleaved away a corner of Shady Springs. "Everyone is made to think that either you cripple the miners or you cripple the community, like it's either/or. But the mines can be run in ways that are fair to everyone, so that neither side is crippled, so both can prosper." She gazed at the mountainous Appalachian skyline beyond. "The ridges around here are ideal sites for windmills, and where coal mining has removed mountaintops, the mine already owns the land and the access roads are built, which are two big costs of such projects. Raising a windmill on a ridge could create as many jobs around here as sinking a mineshaft near a coal seam, and while a coal mine might supply energy for a decade or two, a windmill might supply it forever. And if a windmill suddenly collapsed, three hundred people wouldn't die. Imagine, a living windmill being a tombstone for a dead coal mine. So sad, so stupid."

Another resident angrily said, "When Cain repealed that bill in front of the network TV cameras with all those husky miners standing behind him, some of those men had never thrown a shovel of coal in their lives. Cain also flew them in first class and treated them like kings in his fancy hotel on Pennsylvania Avenue. Fake news? You bet."

When President Cain repealed the Stream Protection Rule, Senate majority leader Mitch McConnell of Kentucky, which has 165 operating coal mines compared to West Virginia's 184, said, "The legislation we repealed today will remove this disastrous rule and bring relief to coal miners and their families." Senator McConnell should now revise his words to say, "The legislation we repealed today will encourage disastrous coal mining practices and threaten death and devastation to local miners and their families."

Of Cain's repealing of the Stream Protection Rule, Senator Devereaux Irksen of Illinois, whose oratory has often rung from the rafters of the Senate, proclaimed: "How can we prick the calloused conscience of this shepherd of our national flock? Only the momentum of millions of moral minds, dedicated to preserving those environmental precepts that underlie our nation's enduring prosperity, can blunt the tip of his impoverishing pen."

Who will be King, coal or the public welfare?

One authority has an answer for this, Trebor Trubel, an environmentalist for thirty years. He said, "Many people believe we need to preserve the environment because it is pretty, so we can enjoy the birds, and hike, and swim, and fish in nature. But environments serve us infinitely more than this: They purify our air, recycle our water, absorb our wastes, modify our climate, and provide a substantial portion of our food and fiber needs without economic cost or human management. We need to preserve environments here, there, everywhere, not so we can enjoy them at our leisure, but so our grandchildren can breathe." If the environment prospers, its inhabitants will prosper.

OVERHEARD IN THE OVAL OFFICE

I'M GETTING SICK and tired of those bastards! Obama's people, Valley's people, Shillery's crowd. Every time I try to think of how to pass one of my bills Cockspur parades another few lawyers in here to discuss another investigation. They're swarming around me like flies!"

"With all due respect, Mr. President, you might have brought some of this strife on yourself. You didn't have to accuse Obama of wiretapping your phone. And you didn't have to say Clarian Valley was showboating during his investigation. And you don't have to keep calling Shillery's crowd sore losers. These are respectable people, and they have many—"

"They're not respectable people!"

"All right, if that's the way you want to see it. But if you keep treating them like a kid poking at a hornet's nest, their many friends around here will sting you when they can."

"I know one way to get rid of em, which is why I asked you to drop over, see if you could help me."

"Me help you?"

"You. You're the military."

"So?"

"So, I know how to get rid of these bastards with the stroke of a pen."

"How's that?"

"Declare martial law! Before they ruin everything."

"And as National Security Advisor, you want me to clear the way?"

"Who else? No more lies, no more fake news. The people I love would be behind me a hundred percent."

"What about the other seventy percent of the country?"

"They can bitch all they want, they can't *do* anything."

"They can have meetings, and march, and demonstrate."

"The people I love will oppose them. If they get a little rough, well—"

"You would condone that?"

"They'd be helping the military, making your job easier. If they get thrown in jail I'll pardon them, full and complete pardon."

"Do you know what the public would think of this?"

"What can they *do?* They'd be a bunch of trapped bunnies."

"Bunnies...they could vote for the Democrats in the mid-terms."

"Not if we cancel them."

"Cancel the elections. The mid-terms?"

"We don't need more elections, just people who'll make this country great again. Martial law, beautiful."

"Mr. President, for many citizens the right to vote is almost a sacred privilege no matter who or what they vote for. Eliminate the mid-terms, and you could have the makings of an insurrection on your hands."

"Wouldn't happen with martial law."

"You'd be surprised if you antagonize them enough. And why go to the trouble? It's easier to quell insurrection of thought than insurrection of deed. If you have nothing to hide, why worry about the investigations?"

"Because they're lies made up by Obama's people, Shillery's crowd, sore losers who want to embarrass my presidency. Besides, people forget, a week after the investigations are dismissed nobody'll remember."

"And you believe I'll lead the charge?"

"You lead the military."

"But force is a confession that discretion has failed."

"People wouldn't care if they kept their jobs, paid less taxes."

"But my leadership is based not on repression but respect. Respect for what our Constitution stands for Americans everywhere, and for billions of repressed people in other nations that we are a dream they embrace."

"They'll dream bigger when America is great again."

"Mr. President, if America is to be great again, it will be so only if we're a nation that others admire. If other nations lose hope in what America stands for, our diplomatic relations with them will weaken, our mutual economic interests will diminish, our sharing of intel will lessen, and our enemies will increase until a few billion people around the world will find ways to overrun our country."

"We have lots of weapons, missiles, planes, ships, beautiful."

"As one who has lived and breathed war for the better part of my life, I can tell you it takes people to launch the missiles and fly the planes and sail the ships. With less than five percent of the world's population, we wouldn't have the feet on the ground to make your idea work. It would take far fewer people to maintain friendly diplomatic relations with the same nations."

"But people forget."

"Not if you offend them deeply enough. If you replace diplomacy with war they'll do anything but forget, and by mid-term elections, millions of voters may so indelibly hate you they'll say I'll vote for anyone but you."

"Not if we cancel the mid-terms."

"Well you won't get me to take your orders, not on this one."

"Then I'll *fire* you!"

"And then?"

"I'll keep firing generals till I find one who does what I want."

"What if Congress won't confirm your nominations?"

"I'll dissolve em. Too many anyway."

"And the Supreme Court?"

"We have a majority there."

"What if they turn against you?"

"Dissolve them too. The military can run everything, beautiful."

"No they won't. Because if you try this, you know what I'll do?"

"What?"

"Mr. President, you may be Commander-in-Chief of the military, and I may be under you and the military may be under me, but this means that I'm between you and the military —and if you try something as monstrous as this, under my direction America's military will stage a coup d'etat and instead of you sitting here in the Oval Office you'll be sitting out there in Pennsylvania Avenue. Because when it comes to the physics of all this, you're nothing but a fat old fart who can't even aim a pea-shooter straight."

"How dare—"

"*And with all due respect Mr. President*, if you think I'll send my storm troopers out on a mission like this and put our guided missiles in your misguided hands, think again. I wouldn't *think* of painting such honorable men in such tyrannical stripes and putting the world at such risk, and I am positive that Congress, and the Courts, and We the People of our glorious nation will be behind me and you'll have nothing but a window behind you. So I advise you to forget the investigations, and forget about badmouthing Obama's people and Shillery's crowd, and forget about declaring martial law, and by lightening your load you'll put more thunder in your step. Have I made myself clear?"

"I'll think about it."

"You damn well bet you'll think about it. You can be sure I won't cover your ass on your 'martial plan' the way I did with the Russian intel issue a few months ago. Like a good soldier then, I stepped before the network cannons and said those optics didn't happen when I knew they had."

"You did the right thing."

"Mr. President, when I say something is false I know is true, it scrapes my conscience. And the next time, you can be sure I'll put protecting my country's Constitution ahead of protecting my country's President."

"I had an absolute right to do what I did."

"The issue isn't whether you had an absolute right to do what you did, but whether you were absolutely right in doing it."

"I want Russia to fight terrorism."

"If you think that by sharing our terrorist intel with them they'll help you with this, let me tell you a little secret if you haven't heard it yet. Russia is our enemy. They would *bury* us if they could. Be sure they'll use our intel against us. Our government has its foibles, but our leaders need to find ways

to strengthen its weaknesses instead of trying to smash every branch of our government to splinters if we don't like some of it. So quit being Whiner-in-Chief and stick to your agenda and put some spring in your stride."

"Hm."

"Another thing, Mr. President. If you don't want the fertilizer to hit the fan on this, I strongly advise you not to mention one word of our chat today to anyone anywhere. Not one person. Not Shilling. Not your closest aides. Not a member of your cabinet. Because if you do, I will have a friendly chat with that person about the good old American way during which my sole objective will be to save your ass. So if we're going to sit in the same foxhole on this, I strongly urge you to press the reset button on your thoughts of ending these investigations before any of our words leak to the public."

"Hm."

"I'm beginning to dislike you Mr. President, and I can't overemphasize that you had better think very very very very hard about all of this. Because in the final analysis, I am sure every member of your darling cabinet, and every member of your cherished Congress, and every one of our honorable federal judges across the land along with a great majority of the American people will back me up on this. Have I made myself clear?"

Silence

"Have I made myself clear!?"

"Get outa here."

"I will do so sir but not in retreat. And say hello to your wife for me."

FROM *THE WASHINGTON POST*:
PRESIDENT WEIGHS DECLARING MARTIAL LAW

L ATE YESTERDAY MORNING President Conan Cain and his U.S. National Security Advisor, Lieutenant General Hammond Taylor "H. T." McManus, discussed the possibility of President Cain declaring martial law as a way of ending several vexing investigations of his activities ranging from leveraging his presidency to make money for his personal businesses to colluding with Russia's Vladimir Putin to win the election.

During their meeting, Cain first said that if he declared martial law he could "Dismiss those bastards [the investigations] with the stroke of a pen." Since this would require the backing of the military, McManus demurringly replied, "And you want me to clear the way for this?"

Cain answered, "The people I love would be behind me a hundred percent," to which McManus rhetorically inquired, "What about the other seventy percent of the country?"

When Cain haughtily responded, "They can't *do* anything about it. They'd be a bunch of trapped bunnies," at such a barbaric remark McManus must have gasped. Yet he evaded any aggressive response and placidly replied, "They could vote for the Democrats in the mid-term elections," to which Cain stated, "Not if we cancel them. We don't need more elections, just people who'll make this country great again. Martial law, beautiful."

At this chilling thought the General replied, "Eliminate the mid-terms, and you could have the makings of an insurrection on your hands."

"Wouldn't happen with martial law," snapped Cain.

"And you believe I'll lead the charge?" the General replied.

"You lead the military," said Cain.

"But my leadership is based not on repression but respect for what our Constitution stands for Americans everywhere; and for billions of repressed people in other nations, we are a dream they embrace."

Cain retorted, "They'll dream bigger when America is great again."

From here McManus' hackles seemed to slowly rise. He replied, "if America is to be great again, it will be so only if we're a nation that others admire," adding that if we don't do this, "it won't take long for a few billion people around the world to find ways to overrun our country."

Said Cain, "We have lots of weapons, missiles, planes, ships, beautiful."

The General now led the charge instead of following it. "As one who has lived and breathed war for the better part of my life," he said, "I can tell you it takes people to launch the missiles and fly the planes and sail the ships. With less than five percent of the world's population, we wouldn't have the feet on the ground to make your idea work. It would take far fewer people to maintain friendly diplomatic relations with the same nations."

At Cain's further insistence McManus finally said, "You won't get me to take your orders, not this time," to which Cain snapped, "I'll *fire* you! I'll keep firing generals till I find one who does what I want," adding if necessary not only will he cancel the mid-terms, he'll "dissolve Congress", and "dissolve the Supreme Court," that "the military can run everything, beautiful."

At these words McManus' hackles must have prickled through his epaulets as he replied, "Mr. President, you may be Commander-in-Chief of the military, and I may be under you and the military under me, but that means I'm between you and the military —and if you try something as monstrous as this, under my direction my military will stage a coup d'etat and instead of you sitting in the Oval Office you'll be sitting in Pennsylvania Avenue." McManus then berated Cain with the ultimate put-down, "When it comes down to the physics of all this, you're nothing but a fat old fart who can't aim a peashooter straight."

The President grew furious —but the General, used to firing in the heat of battle, shot back, "Quit being Whiner-in-Chief and stick to your agenda and put some spring in your stride."

So now we know. America's President would throw over its citizenry the despotic shroud of martial law —if this is what it would take for him to end several vexing investigations that could expose his likely criminal behavior. We also know his National Security Advisor is a true patriot —a *Profile in Courage*— who under the threat of banishment unhesitatingly put Love of Country above licking the boots of an aspiring tyrant.

OVERHEARD IN THE OVAL OFFICE

I THOUGHT WE SAID we wouldn't say a word to anyone about our conversation the other day!"

"I swear I didn't tell anyone!"

"Then why are our words plastered on the front page of every newspaper across the country?"

"I swear I don't know!"

"You swear you don't know. I know I didn't say one solitary word about what we privately discussed to anyone anywhere. That leaves you. Also the quotes in *The Post* weren't the result of word-of-mouth but were recorded."

"We're having trouble with this, my conversations here, with somebody taping them. My SSAs have searched this place everywhere and they can't find a bug or mike anywhere. It's like a bird's taping me from the sky."

"Mr. President, even your closest advisors know you can't let a word out of your mouth without twisting it into a slippery lie. And as surely as I can see the whites of your eyes I will say this is another of your petty pathological lies. An effort to embarrass me, or manipulate me, or put me in an awkward spot, or undermine my efforts to uphold the principles of democracy we supposedly share, or otherwise impugn my integrity somehow. Regarding this tactic of aggression on your part, judging by the stars on my epaulets I too know something about tactics of aggression, and believe me I can employ its ordnance as strikingly and effectively as you."

"I'm not lying about this."

"Saying that you're not cues me that you are."

"I swear I—"

"Mr. President, I once wrote a book, one widely read in military circles, that described how President Johnson and his advisors lied to the public in ways that led to the most wasteful war in our history, and I believe I know the psychology of lying quite well. And with all due courtesy sir, it would be an understatement to say you have a proclivity for reversing reality."

"If you know so much, find who's taping my conversations."

"When I'm convinced you're not lying for the fortieth time, maybe I will."

"I promise I'm not lying about this."

"Mr. President, when you were a kid, did you read the story of *Cry Wolf*?"

"Sure."

"That's what you've become. You've lied about so many things so many times to so many people, if you ever told the truth about anything, no one would believe you."

A PRIMER ON MARTIAL LAW

SIMPLY SAID, martial law is a military takeover of a civilian government. Beyond this skeletal fact, martial law is a fleshy abstraction. As a sample, *what* military takes over *what* government?

Let's take these two *whats* one *what* at a time.

What military? This can be from a foreign country, as when one invades another, or it can be a dissident military faction within a government that overpowers the rest of the military and its civilian government by force.

What government? Its administration or its citizenry? Martial law can involve either or both, and each in part or in whole. Examples? The military could take over the presidency, what is known as a coup d'etat, and leave intact all other parts of a government's operation. Or the military could do nothing more than cancel an election. Or it could shut down all of a government's operation for any length of time, as has existed in many despotic regimes for years, one example being the thirty years of continuing martial law in Egypt. In the United States a brief example of martial law occurred in 2001, when after 9/11 the President as Commander-in-Chief of our nation's armed forces shut down the government and the nation's transportation networks until he was sure we weren't about to be invaded, and a few days later everything returned to normal. Thus martial law can be a vicious oppressor of human rights or a blessed saviour of the same.

Martial law can also be imposed against only a part of a government's citizenry. This occurred in the United States during World War II, when 120,000 Japanese-American citizens were forcibly detained in internment camps. Thus martial law can be imposed on any part of a government's operation or its people, the only rule being that this military action rules when no other social rule can effectively rule in the eyes of its rulers.

However, every declaration of martial law, no matter how short, long, narrow, wide, shallow, or deep it may be, must be backed by a strong military. In this respect, anyone, a president, a general, even you or Rosie McDonnell, could declare martial law on a country as big as the United States, *if* you commanded a military that was strong enough to make your declaration stick.

So that you may acquire a fuller understanding of how martial law could affect you personally, here is a list of its most repressive aspects...

Outlawing of free speech, and control of the media.

Control or elimination of religious services.

Suppression of dissenting literature.

Forbidding public meetings, parades, and other events and activities.

Dusk-to-dawn curfews.

Canceling of elections.

Suspension of the Constitution or any part thereof.

Rationing of essential resources, including food and water.

Confiscating weapons as guns, knives, explosive chemicals, etc.

Seizure of personal assets including property, homes, businesses, etc.

Massive surveillance and "snitch" programs.

Extensive "papers please" checkpoints with intrusive searches.

Roundup of political dissidents.

Forced relocation, and conscription into labor camps and the military.

Imprisonment or execution without due process of law.

FROM *THE NEW YORK POST* CELEBRITY GOSSIP COLUMN:
LINCOLN'S BED NEVER HAD SUCH COMPANY

WASHINGTON— Even though President Conan Cain is betrothed, it seems he still has eyes for any garment that has a pretty woman inside. He reportedly has had a number of dalliances with his attractive Tax Counsellor, Candice Curtiss. A favored tryst is Lincoln's bed down the hall and up the stairs from the Oval Office. One could say the President is keeping a mistress in the White House, well out of view from the lofty lodgings of his lonely spouse in New York. Apparently Ms. Curtiss enjoys the President's digs in more ways than one. Hopefully their labor isn't too taxing on either party.

WASHINGTON — The U.S. Department of Justice's recent investigation of the President Cain's personal finances has determined that he is knowingly and willfully using his office to make huge sums of money for himself and his family. The investigation's Director, Deputy Attorney General Sansome Driver, said, "Since it would likely take years to examine all of Cain's more than a hundred businesses around the world, after investigating twenty-seven of them we know precisely how Cain is using the Presidency to illegally profit from these ventures, and, in the best interests of abridging time, it would serve the public well to disclose what we know now.

"When opening this investigation," continued Mr. Driver, "I said we can examine any business spreadsheet and trace every path of profit and see that each has a clear direction and a defined limit. This straightforward concept works well with honest people. But we quickly learned this investigation would be otherwise. Since its outset, the President, his advisors, and his family have refused interviews we legally requested, they have withheld documents we had a legal right to examine, and in our efforts to trace his profits they have continually led us into mazes of mystery. Due to these obstructions, which we can only assume were meant to keep us from discovering crimes they had committed, we were forced to base our conclusions on circumstantial evidence."

"But basing indisputable conclusions on circumstantial evidence," Driver continued, "is conceptually as easy as learning what you look like by viewing your reflection in a mirror. Similarly, we can mirror the cost of one of Cain's buildings by viewing its reflection in its architectural plans. Indeed, Cain's company performed this labor before constructing any one of his buildings to determine in advance what it would cost to build —in which they counted the amount and cost of every material used, the time to construct every part, every worker's hourly wage, every fiscal expense such as interest on money borrowed to finance the construction, and every environmental and social cost, plus the contractor's profit if s/he would undertake the project. But when we performed this labor on any of Cain's buildings, we had the added advantage of examining any finished construction. After construction is complete, we could similarly estimate the building's operating costs and net profits. Then if we are refused the information we seek or Cain's numbers differ from ours, instead of throwing up our hands in defeat we can produce our own numerical conclusions —and it is for Cain, not us, to prove otherwise.

"For example, if our analysis indicates a certain building would have cost twelve million dollars to construct, and the sparse data we obtained and the altered spreadsheets we were given indicated the building cost Cain twenty million dollars to construct, we could safely assume something corrupt occurred here —such as hidden gratuities, inflated expenses, unlisted refunds, backstairs bargains, bribes, kickbacks, rakes, garnishes, and other unreported remunerations paid to Cain who likely hid them in an offshore account. From here it is the quickest of suppositions to judge how much money Cain is depositing in his pockets that should be deposited in the U.S. Treasury."

"After performing all this labor on twenty-seven of his projects," Driver continued, "we had an accurate picture of what each cost and where its dollars came from and where they went. Our conclusions may be circumstantial, but again, they are as indisputable as learning what you look like by viewing yourself in a mirror, and they certainly aren't fake news."

Below is a sampling of the many ways Conan Cain and his family are using the prestige of his presidency to stuff money into their pockets that belongs to the public. [This lengthy article which included photos of some of Cain's projects covered more than two pages in this newspaper, and it described only 12 of the 27 businesses the Department of Justice investigated.]

☞ In a number of corrupt foreign governments, Turkey, Azerbaijan, and the Dominican Republic to name only three examples, Cain's associates have engaged in bribes, favors, and other corruptions to induce local officials to approve building code violations, permit projects that otherwise would remain undeveloped, and obtain reduced fees and lowered prices for materials and services needed for the projects they develop. Often the mere mention that "this property is owned by the President of the United States" is enough to increase this flow of favors. The Emoluments Clause of the American Constitution expressly forbids the President from accepting any compensation "of any kind whatsoever" from any foreign state.

☞ In many of Cain's foreign businesses he has retained ownership or granted leases in ways that enable his family to profit from the business's operations even if they do not own the property. He also has bribed local authorities to sell at reduced prices large tracts of land he would later develop after he leaves office.

☞ While President, Cain has doubled the membership initiation fees and increased other prices at his Zorrillo-al-Lago Club in Florida, which he calls his "Winter White House". Cain's associates similarly use the prestige of his Presidency to increase the cost of services, meetings, and events held at his properties around the world.

☞ If a foreign dignitary books rooms and events in one of Cain's hotels, such tenancies typically reap thousands of dollars per month, and the dignitary may be introduced to lucrative business contacts and receive political favors from Cain and his associates, for which the guest often expresses his appreciation with unreported gratuities.

☞ Through a bank in the Netherlands Cain launders huge amounts of money deposited by corruptly wealthy people from around the world. "His income from this business alone," said Driver, "could well exceed his profits from all his other global enterprises combined. Such shampooing typically costs 20 to 35 percent of the total amount; so of every four or five billion dollars Cain drycleans he would neatly fold a billion dollars in his pocket. By any moral standard, laundering illegal money is itself illegal. Worse, the sanitized funds are often used to finance the very terrorism, drug trafficking, and other criminal economies Cain claims he is eager to eradicate."

"Cain may say we didn't investigate his projects where corruption didn't occur," Driver said, "but this is not the point. The point is that after investigating 27 of Cain's more than a hundred properties we know America's President is cheating the American public of millions of dollars. If he really wants to lower Americans' taxes, he can deposit his ill-gotten gains in the citizens' bank account, the United States Treasury."

Cain's Chief Council replied, "Our President may have been caught with a few drips of cream on his whiskers, but these savorings are largely sums he received before entering office and are his business alone." This statement is fallacious on its face —because the Department of Justice probed *only* the gallons of rich cream our "Thief Executive" has licked from his chin since he became President. These earnings not only violate the American Constitution, they violate the United States tax code since Cain is not paying taxes on them; and he is doing this willfully which constitutes fraud that the Internal Revenue Service severely penalizes. If the IRS audits "Citizen Cain" as they would any delinquent taxpayer, they would reap a bountiful harvest.

Says Nobel Solon, a fellow at the Brookings Institution and presently a member of Citizens for Responsibility and Ethics in Washington (CREW): "President Cain will not get away with suborning the public's need to his private greed for very long. This is a recipe for scandal. When you get into a scandal, your old friends melt away." Someday when the hard cold winds of conscience may blow, if all goes sweepingly well, the prison the President abhors may comfort him more than the treasure he adores.

OVERHEARD IN THE OVAL OFFICE

 ONAN CAIN: "I can't believe this bastard publicized this shit! —excuse me, darling."

Connie: "That's all right Daddy, if I haven't heard it by now I'm deaf."

Conan: "He's got nothing on us! No numbers, no connections, doesn't say where the money came from, where it went, all nasty lies, bad, fake news!"

Connie: "But Daddy, he described exactly what we did."

Conan: "He doesn't know a thing what we did! There oughta be a *law* against this, I oughta be able to throw him in jail!"

Adam, his older son: "But the media won't think that way. They always play the freedom of speech card, no matter how rotten the things they say."

Conan Junior: "Who cares what the media does? What should we do?"

Conan: "I'll fire that bastard before he eats lunch today. Ooh! vicious lies, fake news! If any member of the media asks you to comment on this, stonewall em, be unavailable, have someone say you're out of the office, anything. How could that bastard make *up* this?"

Connie: "Daddy, I don't think stonewalling them is a good idea. That might make a lot of people think you're wrong, that you're afraid."

Conan: "I'm not afraid of anybody!"

Adam: "Dad, Connie's right. Listen, nobody said this would be easy, the media hates you, they're ruthless and we're seeing that, we're going to be attacked every day, but forget them. Say the money we make has nothing to do with the way people think about us in this country."

Connie: "Certainly not the people you really care about. Okay?"

Conan: "The mutts."

Connie: "Daddy, you shouldn't think of them that way. They're your base, they're who elected you, you should think and say only good things about them. Say you love them, you care for them, even in private. It's a mindset you need to get into, then you'll be okay. Okay?"

Conan: "Okay. I love them, no numbers, no connections."

Adam: "Connie's right. The people who think you're great, your constituents living all over the country, always say you love them."

Junior: "Let them know you can keep your promises and you'll make them great again."

Connie: "Daddy, a lot of people out there love you, they care for you, so don't worry about this one little person. Fire him, get rid of him, but let the American people know, really, he's just a sore loser who wants to hound you from office and keep you from helping them."

Conan: "People forget, it'll blow over."

Connie: "You know how to reach these people, you really can communicate with them, they'll listen to you. Okay?"

Conan: "Okay. I'll offer em more jobs, less taxes."

Adam: "Right, talk about the promises you made to them, lowering taxes, putting people back to work, your health plan, infrastructure, all the things that will make America great again."

Junior: "Things will turn around. It's going to take time, they'll just have to get used to your way of doing things, your pace."

Conan: "My pace."

Junior: "Your pace. As you have done before, you're going to do this at your pace."

Connie: "Daddy, just keep thinking of the people who voted for you, because they believe in you. That's what really matters. Okay?"

Conan: "Okay. Say I love them."

Connie: "Okay Adam?"

Adam: "Okay."

Connie: "Okay Junior?"

Conan Jr.: "Okay."

Connie: "Okay then. Anything else?"

EN ROUTE

THE LEAVES ARE starting to turn. They look lovely this time of year. When I get home though, the driveway will be scattered with them and I'll have to rake them. Ooh, my aching knees! Jocelyn's right, I should hire somebody to do it, maybe one of the high school kids in the neighborhood.' He glances at the dash. 'Oops, low on gas. Station's a few miles ahead.'

As Hod pulls onto the concrete apron before the pumps, near the base of a tall Exxon sign close to the highway parks a truck looking like a small moving van with an opened roll-up door on the back, in front of which stands a farmer before a long table covered with little baskets of vegetables. On the table's corner a small handlettered sign, FOR SALE.

As Hod gasses up the car he occasionally looks over at the table of vegetables and the silverhaired farmer behind, his thumbs hooked in the bibb of his overalls, and the opened door of the van behind, its roomlike storage area tall enough for a man to stand in and half filled with crates.

After screwing the cap back on the tank and holstering the nozzle in the pump Hod, his knees feeling better than usual, strolls over to the table. As the baskets loom larger in his eyes he smiles and waves, "Hi."

"Hello there," the farmer nods and smiles back. His weathered face is etched with wrinkles, his denim overalls are so faded they look like they've seen ten summers of suns.

Hod surveys the rows of berry baskets with slatted wood sides and slits at the corners, their brims bulging with large ripe tomatoes, yellowneck squash, lumpy yams, fat fuzzy peaches, other autumn harvests. He pauses by a basket of fat ripe tomatoes. "How much are these?" pointing.

"Five dollars, sir."

"That include the basket?"

"No-o, that's another five bucks."

"That's a lot for a little basket."

"Takes more trouble to get the baskets than the tomatoes. You'd be surprised how many folks start to walk off with the basket after buying what's in em, till I say it costs extra."

"Well." Hod looks right and left at several baskets of tomatoes. At how red they are. How big they are, how small the spaces between. A decision tentatively made, he touches one's rim. Affirmingly feels the silky red sphere on top. "I'll take this one," reaching in his pocket. "You have a bag or something I can put them into?"

"Right here," lifting a white plastic grocery bag from under the table. "Anything else today?"

"That's it. My wife buys most of our groceries, and it'd be my luck to get something she just bought."

The farmer slides the basket toward the back of the table to the bag's opened top. "You from around these parts?"

"Charlottesville."

"That's forty miles from here. Where you coming from?"

"Washington."

"You work up there?"

"Sort of. I come by here every week or so."

"Lots of crazy things happening in Washington these days."

"You said it." Hod takes a deep breath. "So, what do you think of Cain?"

"Emphatically, "I think he's doing a good job."

"Ooh?"

"He sure knows how to speak his mind. More than most of them silly politicians up there. Why, what do you think of him?"

"I uh, I don't like the way he says things that make people hate each other."

"You don't say…"

"I guess I just did. Hateful remarks like his don't do anybody any good. They consign the hated and unhated to hostile camps, then they'll likely do a lot less for each other if they had the chance, so why do it?"

"Well…"

"Take you and me. If we had good thoughts about each other, we'd probably be friends. But if somebody puts an idea in your head and mine that makes you hate me and me hate you, we're going to think less of each other. And if that happens here and there a few million times across the country, think of how much less everyone'll want to help each other if they had the chance."

The farmer slowly nods.

"Let me give you an example. If I don't like you, I'm more likely to think, screw this guy, I don't care if he doesn't make a dollar all day. But if we feel good about each other, I might look at the side of your truck there and say, you ought to paint big letters on its sides that say FRESH FARM FOOD FOR SALE, letters big enough so drivers coming can see them in time to slow down. See the difference? It's the spirit of the thing. You never know, maybe something good would come of doing things that way, one by one, two by two."

The farmer's eyebrows rise a little.

"If the side of your truck had big letters like that on it, you might sell in three hours what you'd normally sell in eight. Then you'd have five hours left that you could do something else you wanted to do."

A humoring smile graces the farmer's face. He looks at the tomatoes by his hand holding the plastic bag. "Tell you what," lowering the bag as his other hand slides the basket across the table, "have these on me."

"For free?"

"Yessir. The basket too.   Go ahead."

"Why...*thank* you!"

"Like you say," his smile widens, "I reckon it's the spirit of the thing."

FROM *THE WASHINGTON POST*:
CAIN FIRES DEPUTY ATTORNEY GENERAL

WASHINGTON — Shortly before noon yesterday, a grim-faced Clay Cockspur, Press Secretary to the President, read a prepared statement from the podium of the White House press room saying President Conan Cain has dismissed Deputy Attorney General Sansome Driver from continuing his investigation into Cain's finances and terminated the investigation.

"In the sneaky and suppositious manner in which Mr. Driver has been snooping into the President's private affairs," said Cockspur, "he has impeded the President's ability to enact the legislation he has promised the American people, and he has obstructed his family's efforts to conduct business in a manner that is entirely honest and legal. Moreover, Mr. Driver has unconscionably diverged from what he said at the outset would be his intent. Once his deceitful maneuvers became known, the President had no choice but to dismiss Mr. Driver and end the investigation, which wastes American taxpayers' money on a politicized witch hunt conducted by vindictive sore losers."

Mr. Driver responded, "Our Constitution says the President cannot accept any emolument whatsoever from outside his office, yet he is using his office to gain millions of dollars from his businesses with the couth of a fox guarding a henhouse. He has turned the Department of Justice from a protector of the people to his avenging bludgeon, and he has turned the Constitution from his pursuer to his protector. But the Constitution is founded on a higher law: the moral laws spelled in the Scriptures. As such, above the President is the Constitution and above the Constitution are the Laws of God;

and in this celestial order, Cain's governings of me are less than the governings of the Constitution and less still than the governings of the Scriptures. If those in whom these higher laws are entrusted do not enforce Cain to obey them, his greedy appetite for personal gain at the expense of the American people will likely increase with his feeding.

"Also in this investigation," Driver added, "the President has accused me of being sneaky. But I have been dealing with sneaky people, and my sneakiness has been within the law while Cain's sneakiness has been without the law. As a diligent servant of Justice, I pray the public will believe I made the strongest contribution to their welfare that God would allow me to make."

Already the public is making its opinion known at the White House. By late afternoon crowds of clamoring citizens had gathered along Pennsylvania

Avenue shouting anti-Cain rhetoric and waving signs with bellicose slogans. Crowds of the media congregated in the White House press area well into the evening, and lights in the West Wing offices burned late into the night.

FROM *THE WASHINGTON POST:*
F.B.I. REVEALS CAIN'S TIES WITH PUTIN [2]

WASHINGTON — F.B.I. Director Clarion N. Valley has announced that the investigation he has directed has found that prior to the 2016 Presidential election, Conan Cain willfully conspired with Vladimir Putin of Russia to do the following: Russian intelligence will help Cain win the election; Cain will lift sanctions against Russia if he can and consent to Russia's annexing Ukraine and possibly other nations in eastern Europe; and Cain will receive 19 percent of the profits of Russia's largest oil company.

This arrangement was reportedly formulated on April 27, 2016, at the Mayflower Hotel in Washington, D.C., in a meeting attended by Cain and several aides including his campaign manager Howland Thrile, his son-in-law Neville Nisalt, now-White House Chief of Staff Wynton Mastoguet, and now-Attorney-General Bricker Soliminus as well as Russian Ambassador Sergi Askenazi and key figures from Rosneft, Russia's state oil company. A few days after this meeting Cain gave his first foreign policy speech in which he promised that if elected president he would "make a deal under my administration that's great for America but also good for Russia."

The four principal parts of the Cain-Putin collusion are detailed below:

☞ *Russian intelligence will help Cain win the presidential election.* Prior to the election the FSB (the Russian FBI) and the GRU (Russian military intelligence) hacked e-mail servers used by the Democratic National Committee, hacked Shillery Mitten's servers, and released emails that embarrassingly and dishonestly maligned Mitten. Considering the closeness of the election, any inferences that Russia's tamperings reversed the election's result in Cain's favor are valid.

☞ *President Cain will lift sanctions against Russia if he can.* After Russia's intervention in Ukraine in February 2014, the United States and a number of other nations imposed sanctions against Russia and Ukraine. These contributed to the collapse of the Russian ruble and the Russian financial crisis from 2014 to the present.

☞ *Cain will consent to Russia's annexing parts of Ukraine.* In 2014 Russia invaded Ukraine and seized strategic positions in the territory of Crimea, conducted a disputed election in Crimea in which its citizens voted to join the Russian Federation, and annexed Crimea. Armed conflict has since occurred in this region between Ukraine and Russian-backed separatists. Many foreign nations and organizations such as Amnesty International condemned Russia's actions as breaking international law and violating Ukrainian sovereignty.

☞ *Cain will receive 19 percent of the annual profits of Rosneft, Russia's largest oil company.* In early December 2016, a month after Cain was elected president, Russia sold 19.5% of Rosneft's latest quarterly profits presumably to Cain in which a company in Qatar named Gencore received 0.54% as its fee for brokering the deal. How much money did Cain make here? Here is the math: For the fourth quarter of 2014 (the latest quarter that figures are available) Rosneft's total revenues were 91.7 billion U.S. dollars of which $1.3 billion was net profit. 19.5 percent of $1.3 billion is $253 million —in one quarter alone— payable directly to Conan Cain. At this rate his annual pay from this traitorous act would exceed a billion dollars, presumably unreported on his income tax returns. In 4Q 2014 Rosneft's $1.3 billion net income was only 1.4 percent of its total revenues of $91.7 billion. Compare this with Exxon's 4Q 2014 net profit of $32.5 billion which was 8.9 percent of its total revenues of $365 billion. Hence 3Q 2014 was likely a poor quarter for Rosneft; that normally Cain's take-home pay would be far greater.

"Our quadrennial presidential election is the crown jewel of American democracy," said Director Valley, "And based on our findings, I can honestly state that Conan Cain knowingly conspired with a foreign enemy to subvert our democracy's method of choosing our leaders in a manner that reversed the result of our free election —all for thirty pieces of silver. He is a traitor to his country. I would call him a Benedict Arnold, but Arnold's betrayal pales compared to those of Cain. Arnold tried to give West Point to Britain; Cain tried to give America to Russia. One may wonder how could such a terrible person be elected President of this country? The answer? Rig the election!"

Cain's collusion with Putin is by far the most extraordinary abuse of presidental power ever by an American President. In comparison, Harding's Teapot Dome scandal, Nixon's Watergate incident, and Reagan's Iran-Contra affair were thrift-shop pilfers compared to Cain attempting to mug our country of billions of dollars. Despite a barrage of Twitters from Cain saying the F.B.I.'s investigation is all "total lies, vicious fake news, public knows it," Cain's criminal acts undoubtedly comprise "treason, bribery, and other high crimes and misdemeanors" as described in Article 2, Section 4 of the American Constitution —and as such are grounds for impeachment. Make America great again? If only Cain's followers who spout this slogan the loudest would take an honest look at the facts and be the quickest to condemn him.

And what will it take for the Department of Justice to get the wheels of impeachment rolling? This is no easy task when the henhouse of justice is guarded by the foxes of executive privilege and the deliverers of justice are the fox's posse. Yet the ever eloquent Senator Devereaux Irksen addressed this treachery by saying: "From his marble chamber teeming with treason and self-wealth while standing on the shoulders of his pygmy followers, President Cain has launched a new orbit for our nation, one whirling toward self-destruction, one that as it takes its epitaphic course will leave its citizens to molder to maggots and dust, and any echoes of glory will have long since waned. If his treachery continues unabated, the global effects of our noble experiment in governance will diminish to a stain on a page of history, then will be lost forever to cosmic observers from afar. If only he would dispose what his most moral citizens propose."

OVERHEARD IN THE OVAL OFFICE

THAT BASTARD'S GONE PUBLIC with this! (rattle of paper). The son of a bitch! I'll fire his ass before he eats his breakfast tomorrow!"

First voice: "Maybe you better not do that, Boss. Didn't work when you fired Driver last week. It was like pouring gasoline on a fire."

Second voice: "Boss, I feel like we been caught red-handed."

"Red-handed— this is no time for jokes, Howland!"

"I –I wasn't trying to –to joke, I didn't mean the Communists, I –I meant it looks like we've been caught *in flagrante dilecto*, you know, he's described everything we did right there."

"He's described nothing we did right here!" You gotta think like you don't even know the jerk who did this, like you're a different person. For every trick they have we have three, and if they want to play hardball we'll show em our balls are even harder. That son of a bitch! Okay?"

Third voice: "But Boss, they know every phone call I made, every meeting I went to, even in Russia. Things I thought nobody could ever trace. They even know how much money I was paid. I thought it was *laundered*. It's scary!"

"We'll never beat this if you think that way!"

"Then how'm I gonna think about it?"

"Blame it on the vicious sore-loser Democrats, Obama's people, Shillery's crowd. Invent a story in your head, think it over and over till you really believe it, then say it a hundred times until everyone else believes it. Demand to know their sources, say they don't know what really happened because they weren't there and we were. Say the hateful media made it up, every meeting you went to, every word you spoke, every dollar you were paid, all lies, fake news. But we have our own friends in the media, we can invent lies and make em stick as easy as he can. That son of a bitch (rustle of papers). That son of a bitch!"

"But Boss, I don't want to end up in the pokey for ten years."

"You won't end up in any pokey, Wynton. Not even overnight, I have plenty of tools in the box to deal with that."

"Like what?"

"Like if they indite you and make you testify in their politicized witch hunt environment, get your story straight in advance, and when you're testifying act innocent as hell. Plead the fifth if you have to. If they find you guilty, even of perjury, before you've hardly stepped off the stand I'll pardon you, unconditional complete pardon. That son of a bitch! Okay?"

"But I still find it hard to lie about everything."

"Duey, you know to describe these things, you tell him."

"Wynton, you've got the wrong mindset. People love to hear lies! It's like magic: You transform reality for people, you magnify their aspirations, you lift them out of their misery and give them something to live for. Lying is a cheerful affair: It's humor, it's melodrama, it's a sleeping pill that lets one enter the world of dreams and believe in great things, it's the basic ingredient of every fairy tale ever told. It's enough to glorify a lie; but embroidering a lie with coyness only makes it glitter even more, and glossing a lie with solemnity makes it shine like polished gold. It's one thing to relish that feeling —but to share it with another? That's an honor! There's no better way to spread an idea you want everyone to believe than to launch it with a lie."

"Attaboy Duey. If everyone of you does that long enough and hard enough, everyone else will love you. And Floyd…I want a word with you. Don't you *ever* think again of testifying before any federal or congressional committee if they offer you immunity. What you did was dangerous! I nearly crapped screaming worms when you did that. You put everyone's asses here at risk with that, so don't you *think* of going there again. Okay?"

"Okay, boss, you have my word."

"Did I breathe a shitpile of relief when they refused your request for immunity! But we might not be so lucky next time. Whatever dough you might have saved by doing that, when this blows over I'll double it from my own private stock. That son of a bitch! (rattle of paper). The nerve!"

Fourth voice: "What about the Department of Justice?"

"If anyone in Justice appoints a prosecutor who doesn't see things our way, I'll fire his ass. If I have to, I'll keep firing prosecutors till they run out of prosecutors to fire. Each of you sitting here has salted away a good lump on this, when this blows over I'll see you'll get another."

"What if we're indited by a judge you can't touch? Like Sirica during Watergate. He just kept coming. After he ordered the tapes describing the Watergate break-in to be turned over to the prosecutor, Nixon tried the 'fire the prosecutor' routine and it backfired."

"Nixon caved. He should've kept appointing prosecutors till his term ended four years after he was elected."

"But the voters turned against him."

"The voters didn't turn against him, the media *said* they turned against him. Only after the media painted him black did the voters see him the same. And the Dems had a majority in both houses then. Duey, you're good at history, you know how many seats the Dems held in the House and Senate then?

"I believe it was 244 representatives and 56 senators."

"Now it's the other way around, the Republicans own both houses. That's a powerful tool in the box, big difference."

Fourth voice: "But I've seen that change pretty fast."

"Can't change till the midterms. We have plenty of time to turn things around, create more jobs, lower taxes, things that'll make voters forget this piccadillio (rattle of paper) ever happened. Okay?"

Murmur of okays.

"That son of a bitch! Another thing. For the life of me I can't find who's leaking it seems every word we say in here. I've had security comb through every inch of this place, floor, walls, ceiling, furniture, they can't find a thing, no tapes, no mikes, no nothing anywhere. Sometimes I think this room has more bugs in it than Swiss cheese has holes."

"Maybe someone in security is leaking."

"Thought of that. But they make sure everyone there is a true believer."

"Maybe it's somebody outside somewhere."

"Thought of that too. I got squads of security hunting everywhere around here, every building, every floor, but for all the good they've done they might as well be looking for a needle in a haystack in Kansas. If anyone here is leaking what we say, he's the most goddamned sickest lying cocksucking traitor that ever walked the earth. (Rattle of papers). That son of a bitch!"

First voice: "Maybe we should be careful what we're saying now."

"May be. Almost like somebody put a bug in my hair."

Fourth voice: "Maybe get your hair cut, boss, crew cut, real short."

A few laughs.

"Aw, I couldn't do that. People'd think they got a new president. So every one of you, you Howland, Neville, the rest of you, get your stories straight, don't answer the phone, be out of the office, out of town, whatever works."

Second voice: "We'll be quiet as clams under the sand."

"Ha ha, I like that. Quiet as clams under the sand. As for the rest of it, keep your lips tight as a virgin's twat every second of the day. Everyone you work with. Everyone in your family, every friend, no sweet nothings in any pussy's ear late at night. And be careful of the booze. Few drinks and your tongue is wagging like it doesn't know who you are. Okay?"

A few murmurs.

Second voice: "Anything else we should do?"

"Let's see. Prosecutors. Judges. Ministers —get a few ministers on our side. People love ministers, believe every word they say. If any you know any ministers, weep on their shoulders and tell em what we know is the truth, say it's God's truth, tell em to spread the word. Billy Graham, he still around?"

Fourth voice: "All he's doing these days is watching the sky."

"Waiting for the angels to pick him up, too bad, we could use him. Everybody loves ministers. Evangelicals, especially evangelicals, they go for God big time. Those mutts in the Rust Belt and the South will suck in every word, believe everything they say. Evangelicals, good people."

Hod lowers the cane in front of the window and turns off the recorder. "I can't stomach any more."

<hawksbill@gmail.com

GHOST . . . MY GUMSHOES are telling me that soon the Dictraitor's right hand man might do some big things. Could you make me another cane that can detect his voice? I might be onto something here.

<ghost@mirror.com

Hod…It took me three weeks to make the first one but it will take me three hours to make the second. I could have it for you by ten tonight. Down with Dictraitor Cain! Good name.

<hawksbill@gmail.com

Ghost…Don't like driving much at night anymore. Can be there by noon tomorrow if the traffic is light. Okay?

<ghost@mirror.com

Hod…Okay. By the way, it just appeared in the papers that when Clarion Valley received a memo right before the elections last fall saying Shillery Mitten had hidden some classified emails on Anthony Weiner's laptop, that memo was written by Russian hackers. They reversed the election! The winner lost and the loser won! That explains a few things we were guessing about.

FROM *THE WASHINGTON POST*:
AFTER PROBES CAIN'S POPULARITY PLUMMETS

THE LATEST PRESIDENTIAL approval poll conducted by Cantor Survey indicates that since the Justice Department revealed President Conan Cain is using his office to make huge amounts of money and the F.B.I. disclosed his traitorous ties with Russia's Vladimir Putin, the President's national approval rating has plummeted from 37 to 21 percent. The poll's projections are based on phone interviews with a representative sample of 2,000 American adults, and its margin of error is plus or minus 3 percent.

In addition to the 21 percent who approved of Cain's performance, 71 percent disapproved and 8 percent had no opinion. Only 8 percent of Democrats and 13 percent of Independents approved of Cain's conduct, as did 36 percent of Republicans. A 21 percent presidential approval rating is the lowest since Cantor Survey began conducting polls during Franklin Roosevelt's presidency in 1937. Even Nixon's approval rating during the nadir of Watergate bottomed at 24 percent. President Obama's lowest approval was 38 percent, Clinton's and Ford's all-time lows were 37 percent, John F. Kennedy's was 56 percent, and Eisenhower's was 48 percent.

Analysis of Cain's latest approval rating reveals that white, middle class, suburbanite, and educated voters countrywide are deserting him in droves. Newspapers have almost universally condemned him; his campaign contributions from corporations and wealthy individuals are running dry; much of his administration has left (many positions were never filled to begin with); many of his appointees are becoming disappointees as they tender their resignations and head for the exits; and —lest the candle singe the moth— politicians who once licked his boots are fleeing his patronage as if he has the plague. It seems Cain's only loyalists are a close huddle of corrupt cronies who, if justice takes its lawful course, may someday take up residence in a penitentiary.

Even the President himself seems to dig his hole deeper with every effort he makes to climb out of it. His every clamor of fake news only rings as damnable truth, his every attempt to disparage someone only makes him look worse, and his every effort to present himself as providing for the public welfare only seems as if he's picking their pockets instead.

The venerable Senator Devereaux Irksen of Illinois proclaimed, "Cain is making a scarecrow of the Presidency. Instead of fearing away every evil that could prey on our nation's citizens, these evils are seeing through his shabby habiliments and feeding at his feet."

Speaking of feet, Republican Senator John McCain of Arizona unlaced his thoughts with the retort, "Every time we turn around, another shoe drops from this centipede." If all goes damagingly well, someday the centipede may be walking barefoot over a bed of hot coals.

IN STILL ANOTHER DAY of heavy trading, yesterday the Dow Jones industrial average fell another 730 points, or 5.3 percent, closing for the day at 12,946. This is the first time this significant financial indicator has fallen below 14,000 since November 2012. Since the Department of Justice revealed that Conan Cain is using the Presidency to enrich himself and the F.B.I. disclosed his collusive ties with Russia, the DJA has plummeted more than 3,000 points. Last Monday stocks plunged nearly a thousand points, then rebounded slightly upward 115 points on Tuesday, then plunged another 1,050 points on Wednesday before its 730 point descent yesterday.

In the space of two weeks the stock market's historic slide has thrown the world of finance into turmoil and plunged the public mood from glory to gloom. It has halted hundreds of deals in the making, and prompted investors to scour financial portfolios for possible bargains. On Tuesday some corporate raiders, believing the market would bounce back after Monday's stunning loss, began to buy shares on the cheap —but when stocks plunged again Wednesday they quickly sold what they had bought and ended up as sackholders more than stockholders. When falling prices triggered liquidation of programmed portfolios as targeted prices were hit, the plunge only steepened.

Though the Dow Jones Average rose to historic highs during the months after President Cain's inauguration, during the following few months the DJA lost all these gains and more due to a number of Cain's foreign policy decisions that have increased economic instability worldwide, a few being his decision to terminate the Iran Nuclear Pact, his pulling out of the Paris Climate Agreement, his continued insistence that Mexico pay for building a wall along America's southern border, and the Trans-Pacific Pact disaster. Many global nations, including nearly half of the 195 signatories of the Paris Climate Agreement, have expressed disgust at Cain's continued insults and hostile actions toward them and their neighbors, and many are deciding it would be better if they traded with each other rather than the United States.

All of this has led a number of major American companies to pare their forecasts of corporate profits for 2018. A White House official lamented, "We're not sure what to do. It's like trying to lasso a bear in the dark with a string." Said the ever clever Senator Devereaux Irksen of Illinois, "Cain's mal-administrations are robbing our ship of state of monetary ballast and captaining our economy toward committing fiscal suicide. Whenever he swings the Sword of Opportunity in a dissembling effort to aid the public, he only plunges the blade deeper into his own entrails."

One is reminded of how Cain once said he was "smart" because during economic downturns he would wait until prices bottomed then scavenge the fiscal rubble for choice investment nuggets. Could he be engineering the present downturn to create choice investment opportunities for his family? Who's to say these robber barons, sheltered by the highest office in the land, wouldn't try to load their pockets with lucre and lure further favors from their wealthy confreres?

Meanwhile on Capital Hill, the Democrats and Republicans are blaming each other. Even the Republicans find it difficult to get the two wings of their party to flap together, as to each faction the failure of passing what they considered desirable legislation has rotted their once-tasty fruits of victory to wormy apples of discord. If somebody —President, Cabinet, Congress, the Courts— doesn't instill more confidence in our government soon, America's economy may become a bear in a china shop.

OVERHEARD ON CAPITAL HILL

HEY RUFE, I THINK we have a little problem up the road."

"Little?

"Indubitably so."

"About what?"

"About…" (apparently tilting his head toward the White House up Pennsylvania Avenue).

"No…"

"Yes."

"What on earth could be the trouble?"

"Things here n there…like losing millions of voters around the country."

"This is really strange?"

"How so?"

"Because I was just thinking of the same thing."

"What an amazing coincidence!"

"Simply amazing!"

"I wonder if any of our colleagues here might be thinking the same?"

"I move we discuss the matter with the Honorable Senator Ormond Summerland of Texas sipping his favorite beverage over by the bar."

"The motion is carried and further discussion is momentarily curtailed."

Summerland: "Why, it's Vice President Shillin and Senata Stockton Coppitt of Montana. Say, this scotch is goood, eh?"

Shilling: "The Boss isn't the only one who can round up a case of this."

Summerland: "Goes down smoooth as cream on a daince room floor."

Shilling: "It sure goes nice with your Texas drawl, Senator."

Summerland: "Why, thaink you, Rufe. The caviah isn't so bad eitha."

Shilling: "From Russia with love."

Summerland: "Hahaa. Say, you boys seem have somethin on your minds."

Shilling (lowly): "It's about the Boss…"

Summerland: "No-o-o. Were you thinkin…"

Shilling: "Mm hmmm."

Summerland: "Amaizin! I was just thinkin the saime thing."

Coppitt: "What an utterly amazing coincidence that all three of us were doing so!"

Summerland: "Why don't we test this amaizin coincidence on a few more of aur esteemed colleagues heah?"

Coppitt: "I make a motion that we repair to the company of the Honorable Senators Morris Glynn of Iowa, Timbalier Dogge of Mississippi, and Masher Worthstone of Kentucky over by the buffet table. They look a little down in the mouth. Maybe we can cheer them up a little."

Summerland: "Motion carried……

Coppitt: Hello Morris, Tim, Masher. The three of us here were wondering about something."

Glynn: "What's that?"

Coppitt: "It's about the Boss…"

Glynn: "Could it be…?"

Coppitt: "Mm hmmm…"

Glynn: "What a preposterous coincidence! The three of us were discussing the same thing!"

Coppitt: "You too?"

Worthstone: "Of all the subjects in the world, what a pluperfectly undeniable, unequivocal, ineffable, inestimable coincidence that all six of us should be wondering the same thing!"

Summerland: "Mellifluously articulated, Senata!"

Glynn: "I have entertained this subject with a number of our esteemed colleagues here, and the degree of coincidence is simply astounding!"

Summerland: "Altogetha, I would wager that many of aur Republican colleagues would concur that Mr. Shillin heah would make a fi-ine presdent."

Shilling: "Considering your suggestion, the humility of every senator here together is far exceeded by my own."

Summerland: "Rufe, I've always balieved you're the best of good men."

Coppitt: "I'll second that, Rufus. I've felt all along that you'd make a better president than Cain. With your Christian charisma and evangelical oratory, you cut a more moral figure than he ever did."

Shilling: "I am honored and humbled by your compliments."

Dogge: "I'll add my log to the fire. Rufe, you'd be a peach of a president."

Worthstone: "Did you say impeach?"

Dogge: "Ah, heheh, I think I made a typo."

Worthstone: "Whatever may transpire in the near future, I pray our inelastically crass, coarse, crude, and clumsy President will quickly 'resign' himself to the situation."

Glynn: "I wonder what our colleagues on the other side of the aisle would think of this controversy?"

Dogge: "I bet they'd fall for this scheme like a pike for a shiner."

Glynn: "You Southerners are full of aphorisms."

Dogge: "Why not? The customers love em. Fine way to get a point across."

Summerland: "Colorful to say the least, Senata Dogge."

Glynn: "We could let the Democrats lead the way and we'll tag along."

Coppitt: "We'll adroitly lead by clumsily following."

Glynn: "That's the surest way."

Coppitt: "Gentlemen, the hour is moving fast. We must act with alacrity on this matter so vital to our nation's welfare."

Dogge: "Early sow early mow."

Coppitt: "An inestimable encapsulation, Senator Dogge. Mid-terms are less than a year away, and if Shilling here became president soon, he'd have time to clean things up in a charismatically Christian way and let the dust settle by voting time. Then we'll be more assured of convincing a majority of the electorate that our years of selfless labor shall indefinitely continue."

Dogge: "Most likely it'll take a few months to clean the henhouse and get the chickens' feathers preened, then another few months to get em to cluck the way we want em to cluck. Along the way we'll feed em all the corn they want."

Coppitt: "A colloquially concise plan, Senator Dogge. Among our Republican colleagues, let us quietly but surely spread the word."

Dogge: "Yee-haah, we'll make America great again!"

Worthstone: "Considering Cain's colossally clownish, clueless, heedless, shameless, boisterously impulsive proclivities, we couldn't avoid doing this if we tripped over our own shoelaces."

Summerland: "With due courtesy Senata, I believe you've grossly undavalued the situaition."

Coppitt: "Accordingly, I nominate Mr. Rufus Shilling here to be the next President of the United States of America in the very near future."

Shilling: "I am greatly honored and deeply humbled to be so nominated."

Coppitt: "Gentlemen, I move the nominations be closed."

Glynn: "Second the motion."

Coppitt: "I move that this decision be ratified by acclamation. All in favor, say aye."

Chorus of murmuring ayes.

Coppitt: "All opposed, say nay."

Silence.

Coppitt: "I declare this decision to be unanimous in favor of installing Mr. Rufus Shilling as President of the United States of America in the very near future."

Glynn: "Say, here comes the Honorable Senator Ransome Mawe of Iowa."

Mawe: "The way all your heads are bent over your drinks, looks like you're cooking up something. Mind if I eavesdrop a little?"

Coppitt: "It's about the Boss..."

Mawe: "You don't say."

Coppitt: "Why would we lie to you?"

Mawe: "I was just thinking the same thing. What an *amazing* coincidence!"

From *The Washington Post:*
House Weighs Impeaching President Cain

WASHINGTON— In the halls of government on Capital Hill, a number of senior members of the Grand Old party, their eyes gazing into the distant reaches of their crystal balls, are growing deeply concerned over the signals they are receiving from the political hinterlands: that around election time next November, the public's sinking opinion of President Cain's maladministrations could sink quite a few members of the Republican party. Feeling their backsides beginning to roast as if from a rapidly approaching fire, in close conferences with each other these political chiefs are arching their brows and offering liquored winks that their passioned support of the President should be reversed toward the next in line to the Oval Office, the mesmerizing televangelist from Montana, Vice President Rufus Shilling.

Hence it was of little surprise to many when yesterday Representative Nancy Sanibel, Republican of Washington and the House Republican Conference Chairman, introduced a resolution calling for the House Judiciary Committee to investigate the impeachment of President Conan Cain. Representative Sanibel said, "Since he entered office, we have persevered with what seemed were his many missteps due to his inexperience in politics; but I am absolutely aghast at learning of his dealings of self-enrichment and his traitorous relations with Russia. In the best interests of the country, the House should immediately consider impeachment proceedings against him."

Representative Harold Hilton, Republican of Maryland and a member of the House Rules Committee, added, "It seems the most prominent citizen of our government, one who oversees all our other government, has inflicted a serious wound to our body politic. We must swiftly expose the nature and extent of this injury and disinfect it, lest it poison our political tissues so deeply that it could threaten our destruction."

In the wake of all this sudden and undreamed of Republican fervor the Democrats act as if they have found a new life. Four members of the House Judiciary Committee, Representatives Sharon Trout of California, Michael Mandel of New York, Satilla Sapelo of Oregon, and William Hazzard of Louisiana, signed a joint statement saying, "Conan Cain's using the prestige of the Presidency to steal millions of dollars and betraying our country to Russia are by far the most outrageous crimes committed by any American president, and his dismissing Deputy Attorney General Sansome Driver for revealing the truth in the name of the Constitution was a desperate act to hide his crimes that only types them in bold face. The burden is now on Congress to firmly respond to this historic violation of law and insult to the nation's integrity."

Amid these stirrings Vice President Rufus Shilling was always seen to stand quietly in the background, his tall eyes beneath his fiery red hair narrow but searching, a thin smile occasionally appearing on his radiant face. When a reporter prodded for his opinion, he pressed his palms before him in a manner of prayer and grayly called the situation "a great tragedy" and said he was "very much saddened" by it.

Since late last summer, Cantor Survey has been asking Americans, (1) Do you believe Vice President Rufus Shilling would make a good president? and (2) Would you prefer Rufus Shilling as president over Conan Cain? Since Cain entered office, Shilling has generally received notably low ratings from Democrats and notably high ratings from Republicans. But in the last two weeks the percentage of Democrats, Republicans, and Independents who would prefer Shilling as President over Cain has rocketed from 39 to 66 percent.

Apparently the winds of change are beginning to sweep across the political hinterlands. What might a political weatherman forecast for the morrow?

A Primer on Presidential Impeachment

Now that Congress is weighing the possibility of impeaching President Conan Cain for certain high crimes and misdemeanors he may have committed while in office, so the public may have a clearer understanding of how this process unfolds, here is a primer…

In our government the portal to impeachment is the House Judiciary Committee (HJC), an assembly of 41 prominent Representatives who essentially act as the lawyer for the whole House. The HJC will vote to impeach the President of the United States if they determine that he has violated either one of two sections of the American Constitution, as follows:

1. *Article 1, Section 9, Clause 8*, states: "No person holding any office of profit or trust under them shall without the consent of the Congress accept any present, emolument, office, or title, of any kind whatever, from any king, prince, or foreign state."
2. *Article II, Section 4*, states that the President "shall be removed from office on impeachment for, and conviction of, treason, bribery, or other high crimes and misdemeanors."

Impeachment of the President is a lengthy legal process because…

☞ Each of the 435 Representatives and 100 Senators is given ample opportunity to fully debate the merits of the President's alleged crimes.
☞ The process is hindered by lack of precedent and unclear language.
☞ The HJC, though theoretically impartial, has partisan proclivities. This is because its 41 Representatives have about the same ratio of

Republicans and Democrats that exists in the House of Representatives; so, since the House's 435 Representatives presently include 247 Republicans and 184 Democrats, the HJC's 41 members include a similar ratio of 24 Republicans and 17 Democrats. Only if the President's behavior is extremely detrimental to many Republicans would a majority of the present ratio of representatives move to impeach him.

The impeachment process begins when one or more persons, known as the Declarer, prepares a *Charge of Impeachment* which alleges that the President has committed one or more crimes in violation of either the Emoluments clause or the High Crimes clause of the American Constitution. The Declarer can be any American citizen of good standing, you for instance, who after preparing your *Charge of Impeachment* delivers it to your local representative in Congress, who after due consideration would bring it to the attention of the HJC. However, if your charge is based on your extreme discontent at something you heard or read that the President has done, your Congressor will dismiss your allegation as lacking substance. But say that while employed as an aide to the President you saw him commit a serious crime, and you have photos, written documents, and taped conversations that prove what you saw. Then your Congressor would likely deliver your *Charge of Impeachment* to the HJC for serious consideration. Here you would appreciably increase your clout if you are any of the authorities or organizations listed below...

A member of the United States House of Representatives.
A federal judge.
A federal grand jury.
A state or territorial legislature.
A special prosecutor appointed by the federal government.
A petitioner who has prepared a formal written request signed by many
    aggrieved people in a certain region or jurisdiction.

When the HJC receives what it considers a legitimate *Charge of Impeachment*, it conducts a private hearing during which it examines the evidence and hears the testimony of any witnesses, who may be cross-examined by each member of the HJC and the President's counselors, then the HJC votes on each count whether or not the President should be impeached. If a majority votes *yea* on at least one count, the HJC prepares a *Resolution to Impeach the President* and sends it to the full House of Representatives for deliberation. After its members debate and possibly revise the issues, they vote on each count.

If a majority votes *yea* on at least one count, the House returns the *Resolution* to the HJC to draft the *Articles of Impeachment*. The HJC then debates each count, now called an *article*, then drafts a document whose wording will hold up in court, and after a mostly perfunctory vote on each article returns this document to the House. Its members again debate the issues, now paying less attention to their content and more to their legal implications, then vote on each article. If a majority votes *yea* on at least one article, the President is officially impeached, and the *Articles of Impeachment* is delivered to the Senate for trial.

The House next appoints a group of House Managers, who essentially act as prosecuting attorneys in a criminal trial, and the Senate issues a writ of summons to the President informing him of the date when he must appear to plead his case. The President may appear alone, be accompanied by counsel, or choose not to appear in which case the trial proceeds as if the defendant pled "not guilty". Theoretically the President could declare martial law and abolish the trial —but this would create such an uproar that no branch of government —military, congress, judges, even members of the President's cabinet— would likely comply. When the pleadings have concluded, the Senate conducts the trial in a courtroom-like setting during which the House Managers and their attorneys represent the prosecution, the President and his counselors represent the defense, the Chief Justice of the Supreme Court presides as judge, and the members of the Senate sit as the jury. At least two-thirds of the Senate must be present. After hearing the evidence, examining witnesses, and considering the closing arguments, the Senators deliberate in private. On each article each Senator votes either *yea* to convict the President and remove him from office, or *nay* to acquit him and allow him to remain in office. Each article requires a two-thirds majority to convict. A Senator who abstains but is present effectively votes for acquital, while a Senator who is absent has no vote either way.

If the President is convicted on one or more of the *Articles of Impeachment*, he is removed from office and is succeeded by the Vice President; or if there is no vice president, whoever is next in line to succeed the President, beginning with the Speaker of the House of Representatives. The Senate needn't vote on all the Articles. If the President is convicted on one or more Articles, the Senate may decide not to vote on the remaining ones; or the opposite may occur: If the President is acquitted on one or more Articles, the Senate may decide it is unnecessary to vote on the others.

Since our nation's founding, the House Judiciary Committee has voted to impeach three presidents.

The first was Andrew Johnson in 1868. In his trial the *Articles of Impeachment* included 14 counts. With 36 votes needed for conviction on any one count by the then-54 members of the Senate, after voting 35 to 19 on the first three charges —one vote short of the two-thirds needed for conviction— the Senate decided it would be a waste of time to vote on the remaining counts.

The second was Richard Nixon in 1974. After the HJC prepared the *Articles of Impeachment* against him, Nixon resigned when faced with a collapse of support in the Senate.

The third was William Clinton in 1999. In his trial the *Articles of Impeachment* included 2 counts relating to his affair with Monica Lewinsky, one on perjury, and one on obstruction of justice. With 67 votes needed for conviction on either count, the Senate acquitted him of perjury with a vote of 45 *guilty* to 55 *not guilty* and of obstruction of justice with a vote of 50 to 50.

After voting, the Senate enters a judgment on its decision and a copy is filed with the Secretary of State. If the president is removed from office, he may be barred from holding any future government office and may be liable to criminal prosecution.

From *The Washington Post:*
House Judiciary Impeaches President

WASHINGTON— After hearing the evidence for three long weeks, until late at night each weekday and all day each Saturday, early last evening the House Judiciary Committee (HJC) recommended that President Conan Cain be impeached for committing a number of high crimes and misdemeanors while serving as President of the United States. The final vote was 32 *yea* to 9 *nay* in favor of impeachment. Of the 24 Republicans on the committee, 15 voted *yea* and 9 voted *nay*; of the 17 Democrats, all 17 voted *yea*.

During these often acrimonious proceedings, the Democratic and Republican members of this respected committee took evidence and listened to the testimony of witnesses concerning the 17 counts listed in the *Resolution to Impeach the President*. As the debating raged it often seemed the busiest person in this august chamber was the Sergeant at Arms. On several occasions he had to separate a pair of honorable attendees who would rather debate their differences with their fists than their tongues.

During these deliberations, Representative M. Morgan Owen of South Dakota commented, "For years we Republicans have campaigned against corruption and misconduct. Now we must prove to the public that we practice what we preach." And Democratic Representative Marion Minnion of New Jersey called Cain's collusive relation with Vladimir Putin of Russia "the most treasonous act ever committed by an American president. What Cain has done in the name of Democracy would betray our government to our greatest global adversary. At the very least the House should immediately investigate the merits of impeaching the President."

On the other hand, Republican William Boister of Tennessee defended Cain with caustic stridency, constantly heaping scorn on anyone who would suggest impeaching the President. At one point during the hearings Boister angrily pointed a quivering forefinger at Chairman Hilton Pinckney and said, "Please do not bore the American public with your incessantly secessionist behavior! Would you demote a man who has worked hard all his life to earn the wealth he now has and has become a prominent example of how other citizens can industriously achieve the same, and whose rallies have been attended by mobs who unlawfully try to disrupt him—"

"They were not unlawful mobs," shouted Representative Howard Glade of Oregon, "they were honest citizens who were exercising their right of freedom to assemble!—"

"Not the way they were doing it!" Boister shot back.

However, everyone in this august chamber would later agree, the heat of acrimony decidedly cooled toward civility with the passioned plea of Representative Ravenna Starling, a woman of color from Texas, who spoke:

"Mr. Boister, you have referred to your adversaries' behavior here as 'Secessionists'. I would like to juxtapose what you call the secessionist behavior of those who propose the President's impeachment with some proclamations that our forefathers made when they were constructing the foundations of this great nation. Regardless of our possible differences concerning the issues being debated here, we all know that certain things President Cain is alleged to have done are obvious. We all know he has refused to divest himself of his business interests while still serving as President. This is obvious. We all know he has done this.

"Now hear what James Madison asserted during the Virginia ratification convention in 1788. 'If the President be connected in any suspicious manner with any person for purposes of personal gain and there is grounds to believe that he will shelter him, he may be impeached.' Time and again newspapers, magazines, and, alas, former Deputy Attorney General Sansome Driver, have spoken of the many emoluments the President has received under the shelter of his business interests. These offenses are obvious. We know they happened. So by forefather Madison's words, these offenses committed by the President are impeachable. How could any moral member of this chamber disagree? Or set these offenses aside as being irrelevant to the case?

"And hear the words of Justice Joseph Story, who served on the Supreme Court of the United States from 1811 to 1845: 'Impeachment is intended for occasional and extraordinary cases where a superior power acting for the whole people fails to protect their rights and rescue their liberties from violations.' Again, time and again, newspapers, magazines, and F.B.I. Director

Clarion Valley have described how President Conan Cain has betrayed our citizens' liberties by making a deal with Vladimir Putin of Russia that Cain would lift sanctions against Russia and ignore its annexing Ukraine in exchange for Russia tilting our national election in Cain's favor and paying him hundreds of millions of dollars. We know these things Mr. Boister. We know they happened. So by forefather Story's words, these offenses committed by the President are impeachable. Again, how could any moral member of this chamber disagree, or set these offenses aside as being irrelevant to the case?"

"Here it is pertinent to ask, why is all this so relevant in light of the present debate? It is this, Mr. Boister. When faced with the tensions of the day, it is exceedingly difficult for one to imagine what life was like in this nation more than two long centuries ago, when our citizenry in the space of one decade became manacled by a repression administered from the far side of the Atlantic. When *We the People* finally said we have had enough, it took seven long dreadful years of bitter war to restore the freedom they once enjoyed. Imagine our citizenry today having to endure that same dreadful span of shackling and slaughter all over again!

"Here our forefathers had an advantage over us: They learned of freedom by having to endure its opposite. As such we do not know it so well, so we are not so aware of its benefits and what we would lose by their absence. But we can learn much of our forefathers' sufferings by reading their histories and experiencing by association how they struggled to replace the fright of repression with the joy of freedom. Then *We the People* of today may come to ask: Is the mere removal of one evildoer so small a price to pay to discourage years of horror involving millions of our numbers from happening again? *This* is what we representatives of our citizenry have been deliberating for three seemingly long but in the great scheme of things three very short weeks.

"So I end by saying to all of my esteemed colleagues seated in this august chamber: Several years of history may be condensed to a page in a book, but history is written every day, and today is one of its epochal days!"

From this point on no fractious clamor resounded from the chamber's walls, only solemn discussions concerning aspects of the president's behavior. Everyone later agreed that Ravenna Starling's oratory turned the tide of the HJC's deliberations from acrimony to concordance, from recalcitrance to deliverance, and reversed the opinions of a number of its members.

Near the conclusion of the deliberations the HJC, to simplify the application of justice, combined all 17 counts of the *Resolution to Impeach the President* into one comprehensive count allegedly committed by the President. Representative Dewey Cumberland of Louisiana expressed the sentiments of many when he said, "Since it seems that most every member of this committee and indeed Congress at large believes Cain either committed all the alleged crimes or none, we needn't repeatedly rattle our sabres for possibly months regarding his multitudinous business operations and numerous aspects of his collusive relation with Putin." Hence the HJC resolved that the *Resolution to Impeach the President* will consist of only one count.

As such, this resolution places the integrity of Cain's presidency squarely on the dock of justice. If the President is truly innocent of the charge, he should welcome this scrutiny and freeing of public opprobrium it would bring. Next the HJC will send the *Resolution* to the full House for deliberation. Much partisan arguing among its 435 members is expected there.

OVERHEARD IN THE OVAL OFFICE

THOSE BASTARDS! What do they know about anything?"

"Easy, Boss."

"If they go through with this, I will *never* resign! Never! I'll suck this job for every dollar I can get till they cart me away in a casket! Besides, if I resign, people would think I did what the hateful media said."

"Boss, if you'll cool off for a moment, we have a way to deal with this."

"What's that?"

"So what if they impeach you?"

"So what!? They could throw me in jail that's what! I swear I will never resign! And if they convict me I'll appeal. I swear I'll find a way."

"You'll need a little help with that, Boss."

"That's what I have you for."

"And it's a good thing you do. Because as your Chief Legal Counsel it is my bounden duty to aid you in these respects as ably as I can."

"So if they convict me, how can I appeal?"

"To begin with, if the Senate convicts and you appeal, I'm sure your adversaries will cite *Article I, Section 3*, of the Constitution that states: 'The Senate shall have the sole Power to try all Impeachments.' But in any trial in our legal system, the defendant can appeal on the grounds that the prosecution didn't adhere to the standards of impeachment as defined by law."

"How would that work?"

"In any court, when someone is tried for committing a crime, the crime is defined in a statute, and if during trial the crime is not adjudicated as defined in the statute, the defense has legal grounds to appeal."

"Hm."

"So our reasoning would be that as surely as a law exists for impeaching a President, if that law is improperly adjudicated during trial, you as surely have a right to appeal on the grounds that the prosecution didn't adhere to the standards of impeachment as defined by law. That's a fundamental legal concept, one defense lawyers go to sleep with every night."

"Hm, hm."

"There's even a legal precedent for this. During Nixon's impeachment, Supreme Court Justice White said: 'Were the Senate to convict the President without a trial, it hardly follows that the Court ought to refrain from upholding the Constitution in such cases.' And during Clinton's impeachment Justice Souter said: 'If the Senate were to act in a manner seriously threatening the integrity of its results, judicial interference might well be appropriate.'"

"You're as good as Roy Cohn was on this. You ever know him?"

"I did, but let's don't get sidetracked. Also, since impeachment proceeds through several stages, and since at each stage the charges might vary slightly from the initial allegations, we can exploit any variances or blunders they make, and constantly claim the prosecution's evidence is prejudiced against the defendant and as such is a violation of your fair trial rights. We could get the prosecution so tied in knots they couldn't think straight. Remember, you always have a right to a 'fair trial,' ho, ho. We could keep the whole thing going for months right there."

"Good, good, every day I sit here I could make another million dollars."

"We can also claim the House Judiciary should have listed each allegation in the *Resolution to Impeach* as a separate count instead of bunching them into one count."

"The sun's coming out, Duey. What else?"

"If the Senate holds the trial, when you're summoned to plead your case you could appear without counsel. Then if convicted you could claim you weren't properly represented by legal counsel when you pleaded your case."

"I like it, beautiful."

"Even if the retrial upholds the original verdict, it'll likely take several months. If we're diligent there's no telling how long we can stretch it."

"Money, money, lots of money."

"Defense attorneys always have an advantage in such scenarios, because while the prosecutor must adhere to the one possible truth, the defense can often find twenty ways to skirt it with deceptions, sidetracks, and outright lies; and the defendant is always 'innocent' until proven guilty. Just because this has never happened doesn't mean it couldn't happen."

"Lots of reasons, beautiful."

"Not only would you set a historical precedent by being the first sitting president to be convicted of impeachment, you would take this precedent a historical step further by appealing your conviction. You'll certainly get a lot of attention, since the media loves this sort of thing."

"For once I'll love em, beautiful."

"Also, if you never resign, even if you're convicted and removed, your core group will think you're a hero, then you can incite them to do almost anything you want."

"Beautiful, beautiful! Duey, if things work out like this, I'll give you a house in the Hamptons for this."

"A box of chocolates would be enough."

"That and more! You're the one person I can talk to about these things."

"You'll make America great all over again."

"Many times, beautiful."

"So when the crowds start yelling *impeach*, don't get rattled."

"I won't, I won't. I will never resign! Never, never in a million years!"

"I'd limit it to eight if I were you."

"I can see that money rolling in! Beautiful."

FROM *THE WASHINGTON POST:*
CAIN'S SECRET IMPEACHMENT STRATEGY

WASHINGTON— In the Oval Office yesterday President Conan Cain and his Chief Legal Counsel, Duey McDougall, discussed how to deal with his impeachment if it should proceed from accusation to conviction. Their central strategy would be for Cain to stay in office as long as he can so he can rake in as much money as possible. As Cain trenchantly exclaimed: "I'll suck this job for every dollar I can get till they cart me away in a casket!"

Their essential strategy would be as Cain asserted, "I will never resign! Every day I sit here I could make another million dollars." McDougall detailed several ways they could prolong his impeachment trial, saying, "Defense attorneys always have an advantage because while the prosecutor must adhere to the one possible truth, the defense can find twenty ways to skirt it with deceptions, sidetracks, and outright lies."

But the nerviest part of their strategy is that if Cain is convicted, he will appeal the verdict! McDougall said, "As surely as a law exists for impeaching a President, if that law is improperly adjudicated during the trial, the accused has a right to appeal on the grounds that the prosecution didn't adhere to the standards as defined by law." McDougall added, "Just because this has never happened doesn't mean it couldn't happen."

What more proof do *We the People* need to know that America's President is stuffing his pockets at public expense and is obstructing every effort of justice to stop him? How long must we wait until justice will finally prevail?

From *The Washington Post:*
HOUSE VOTES TO IMPEACH CAIN

WASHINGTON— Yesterday the House of Representatives, after deliberating until seemingly no wind remained in a single member, voted to impeach President Conan Cain for committing high crimes and misdemeanors while in office. The final tally: 337 *yea*, 64 *nay*, and 34 absent or abstaining. Here and there, one could hear murmurings that a surprising number of Republicans voted *yea*. Nearly 200 members rose to either acclaim or excoriate the accused, quoting everyone from Confucius to Cain himself.

Those in favor of acquittal constantly tried to divert the debate from the traitorous Cain/Putin conspiracy toward Cain's family businesses, claiming they "are not matters of public concern," because, "They do not threaten the national interests the president is sworn to uphold."

Those in favor of impeachment took a different tack. Mostly they remained primly calm under the onslaught of the opponents' fiery assertions, knowing they likely had a ruling majority. Lest the momentum turn against them, one occasionally rose to emphasize Cain's traitorous collusion with Putin, asserting that according to the Constitution "the President has committed treasonous high crimes against the People of the United States."

The *Resolution* will next be returned to the HJC for purposes of drafting the *Article of Impeachment* before it is presumably sent to trial.

From *The Washington Post:*
PRESIDENT CAIN IS IMPEACHED

WASHINGTON— Yesterday, after hearing days of sworn testimony and finally fitting the *Resolution's* paper jaws with sharp teeth by crafting it into a legal document whose words will hold up in court, the House Judiciary Committee officially voted to impeach the President of the United

States. The final vote was 33 *yea*, 8 *nay*. Of the 24 Republicans, 17 voted *yea* and 7 voted *nay*; of the 17 Democrats, 16 voted *yea* and 1 voted *nay*.

As a rare solemnity reigned over the proceedings, each member wrote on a piece of paper, folded the paper, and slipped it into an envelope bearing his or her name on the front. An aide carrying a wicker basket once owned by Betsy Ross paused by each member to collect the envelopes, then the aide carried the basket brimming with the votes to Chairman Hilton Pinckney. Flanked by two aides, Pinckney tallied the ballots.

"Not even close," commented Representative Orion Tremain of Idaho. The final vote seemed a mere formality to what already seemed obvious. As one looked around the room now pervaded by a convivial gaiety, one could fairly tell by a few glum faces here and there who voted *nay*.

The President of the United States is now officially impeached. In recent weeks the fringes of his constituency have grown ever more frayed, with a rumor of marital infidelity on his part occasionally oozing out of the woodwork. It seems the only way he knows how to respond to his accusations is with another terse twitter. Of this practice the ever eloquent Senator Devereaux Irksen of Illinois retorted, "Lincoln's Gettysburg Address contained 1,450 letters while Cain's addresses never contain 140. His titillating sorties brand him as a brazen "pressititute" who shamelessly displays his morals in degrading ways, often with 'beautiful' tagging along in irony as the last word."

Henrietta Frederick, a moderate Republican from Wisconsin, said she finally decided to vote for impeachment. "I came to believe that if we failed to impeach the President for his many crimes, we would stamp on our highest office a standard of conduct that is unacceptable. Indeed, it seems the more Cain tries to wiggle out of his problems, the more he worms into them."

Representative Jeremiah Jekyll of Texas quipped, "Any seventy-year-old who heavily peroxides his hair must have serious self-esteem problems along with all the anxiety and lack of social skills that goes with it. I would feel the same if my teenage grandson peroxided his hair."

Representative Emerson Calmer of Michigan expressed the feelings of many when he said, "From here on, Cain will make it easier for everyone, Congress and citizens alike, if he resigns."

Law professor Solomon Earnheart, who during the HJC's deliberations testified as an expert on the doctrine of executive privilege as exercised by the President since he entered office, played a significant role in undermining Cain's constitutional arguments.

The *Article of Impeachment of the President of the United States* contains one comprehensive count that articulates both the President's receiving numerous emoluments from his businesses and his traitorous collusion with Putin of Russia. Below appears the *Article* en toto....

ARTICLE OF IMPEACHMENT ENACTED BY THE HOUSE OF REPRESENTATIVES OF THE UNITED STATES OF AMERICA IN THE NAME OF THE PEOPLE OF THE UNITED STATES OF AMERICA AGAINST CONAN TYBEE CAIN, PRESIDENT OF THE UNITED STATES OF AMERICA, IN MAINTENANCE AND SUPPORT OF ITS IMPEACHMENT AGAINST HIM FOR HIGH CRIMES COMMITTED AGAINST THE PEOPLE OF THE UNITED STATES AS INDICATED BELOW:

Article 1: High crimes committed by the President, including the crime of secretly receiving numerous emoluments from foreign individuals and agencies through the operation of his many business activities around the world; and including the crime of treasonously conspiring with a foreign adversary, Vladimir Putin of Russia, in a manner that has betrayed our nation to our enemies and undermined our democratic government's system of choosing its leaders through free and fair elections. In committing these crimes while serving as President of the United States, Conan Tybee Cain has violated his constitutional oath to faithfully execute the duties of his office, he has undermined the integrity of his office, he has brought disrepute to the Presidency, and he has acted in a manner subversive of the rule of law and justice, all to the manifest injury of the people of the United States.

Wherefore, Conan Tybee Cain, by such conduct, warrants impeachment, trial, and removal from office and disqualification to hold any future office of honor, trust or profit anywhere in the United States of America.

The *Article of Impeachment* will now be sent to the full House of Representatives for final approval. "This should proceed rather quickly," said Majority Chairman Winston Burnett of Virginia, "since the full House will essentially rubber-stamp an action previously taken by the Judiciary." He said the Senate trial should begin within three weeks, but it may be two months before the Senate renders a verdict.

Due to the rising winds of discontent, it seems the political weathervane is veering ever more toward realistic and conclusive change.

FROM *THE WASHINGTON POST:*
CAIN CLAIMS HE WILL NEVER RESIGN

WASHINGTON— Yesterday afternoon President Conan Cain, with his wife and his five children by his side and his closest Republican colleagues huddled around him, appeared on the South Lawn of the White House before a podium bristling with microphones to comment on the House Judiciary's *Article of Impeachment* now before the House of Representatives.

"On behalf of the American people, people that I dearly love," said the President, his voice husky with rancor, "not only the people in our nation's heartland but even on the east and west coasts, I am terribly disappointed that the House Judiciary Committee has decided to impeach me for certain misdemeanors that, as they are written in their *Article of Impeachment*, are hateful lies. They said nothing about the incredible progress that has been made in this country since my inauguration. We have made incredible progress, all kinds of progress, and they ignored that. Instead they caved under tremendous pressure from the hateful media, the dishonest press, especially in Washington and New York, who continue to say lies about me, who do not speak for the people of this country. The level of dishonesty is out of control, it's a tremendous disservice, all lies, fake news.

"I'll give you some examples of the media's lies. They once said I talked to David Duke. I never talked to David Duke in my life. A nasty lie, all bad.

"They said I discussed with my oldest children how we could use the office of the Presidency to, as they say, fill our pockets with money. Since I've been

President, I never talked to my family about how we could use my office to make money for us in our businesses. All lies, totally misrepresented.

"They said I have called the people in this country who work the hardest and earn the least, who the previous administration left behind, people I dearly love, the hateful media said I called them mutts. I never called them that, never. Such lies, such hatred.

"They said I have slept with Candice Curtiss, one of my Assistant Counsellors, strategist, very capable woman. I never touched her the way the hateful media says. I look at my wife and children here before you today, before the American people, and say I never did such a thing, all complete lies.

"They said I want to remain in office as long as I can so I can make as much money as possible while I am President. I never said anything like that, never, so dishonest, so disgraceful. I've never seen more dishonest media.

"I don't even know where the media got all those stories in the first place, the exact opposite of the truth. I mean they are absolute lies, so much is fake. Something that should be positive, they'll make it negative. As for the possibility that I will resign, I will never resign. As I have done since my inauguration, I will continue to faithfully perform my duties as president of this great nation until my term's final hour."

During President Cain's press conference he said, "I don't even know where the media got all those stories in the first place." Well, Mr. President, this newspaper will tell you where the media got them in the first place. Since you entered office, *The Washington Post* has received from a highly regarded source a number of recorded Oval Office conversations of you with your colleagues and your family. Soon this newspaper will post on YouTube these "Smoking Gun" recordings as audios, then the whole world can hear and know what you actually said. Several passages from these tapes that contradict what you said in your press conference yesterday appear below. Mr. President, compare these actual recordings with the allegations you made yesterday. Mr. and Mrs. America, perhaps you would like to compare them too...
Cain's allegation... "I swear I never talked to David Duke in my life."
Actual recording... "David? This David Duke?...The President of the

United States, that's who it is."

Cain's allegation... "Since I've been in office, I never talked to my family about how we could use the Presidency to make money for us in our businesses."

Actual recording... [The President's daughter Connie Cain] "But Daddy, he [former Deputy Director Sansome Driver] described exactly what we did."

Cain's allegation... "They said I called the people in this country who the previous administration left behind, said I called them mutts. I never called them that, never."

Actual recording... Connie Cain: "Not with the people you really care about. Okay?"
Conan Cain: "The mutts."
Connie Cain: "Daddy, you shouldn't think of them that way."

Cain's allegation... "I never touched Candice Curtiss the disgusting way the hateful media says."

Actual recording... Curtiss: My nylons are terribly clingy."
Cain: "Takes a man's touch."
Curtiss: "You said it, brother. Ooh, your hands are so soft."

Cain's allegation... "I never said I want to stay in office so I can make as much money as possible while I'm President."

Actual recording... "I'll suck this job for every dollar I can get till they cart me away in a casket!"

Hopefully "Citizen Cain" will soon be brought to justice for his many crimes against his country; then perhaps, once and for all, this serpent of greed will be slain in his den.

WASHINGTON— After a whirlwind of vote-counting, last Saturday the House of Representatives overwhelmingly cast their ballots in favor of approving the *Article of Impeachment of the President of the United States.* The final tally? 364 *yea*, 53 *nay*, with 16 absent or abstaining. Of the 238 Republicans, 192 voted *yea* and 46 voted *nay*; of the 195 Democrats, 188 voted *yea* and 7 voted *nay*. Nearly everyone agreed that since *The Washington Post* placed several "Smoking Gun" recordings of President Cain's Oval Office conversations on YouTube last week where they quickly went viral, these live conversations between Cain and his conspiring cronies and his children have quashed his remaining hopes of being acquitted of the *Article*'s charges.

Many of the nation's newspapers have clamored for Cain to step down. *The Providence Journal* wrote, "These living conversations have politically destroyed President Conan Cain. They demonstrate beyond a wisp of doubt his pathological effort to use his office to make money and that he illegally gained that office by betraying our democracy to Russia."

House Majority Leader Wilson Gidea expressed the attitude of many when he said, "These actual conversations of Cain reveal a disgustingly immoral behavior by our nation's leader. If he was his own ten year old child, he would severely punish him for what he has done."

After listening to the tapes Republican Ronald Wiggins of Kansas said, "Due to the President's criminal conduct revealed in these conversations, I can no longer in good conscience vote to acquit him, and I urge my colleagues to do the same. The legislation he hopes we will pass now reeks of self-gain, and surely Congress will carry out his proposed bills on a stretcher."

Said Melinda Fait, a housewife from Concordia, Missouri, "It scorches my conscience that during his press conference last week, he repeated those lies with a straight face before his wife and children!"

But Claude Balls of Montana, an adamant ally of Cain, defiantly said, "Our founding fathers created a government of men, not of angels." His face reddened with emotion as he added, "No member of this House today can pass a puritanical test of piety that some are demanding of our elected leaders. If such demands are met, our seats of government will lay empty and we will see the ablest of our citizens unfairly cast out of public service."

At these assertive words the irrepressible Senator Devereaux Irksen of Illinois countered: "The labor of our esteemed Senators is a perishable commodity: A pair of shoes undelivered on receipt of purchase may be delivered on the morrow; but a verdict of guilt undelivered on receipt of testimony of the President's willfully committed crimes will be lost forever. Such dereliction of duty would forever taint the integrity of our nation's lawmakers, and besmirch our histories that would be read by our childrens' children."

After the votes were tallied and clusters of representatives chatted with their colleagues here and there in the chambers of the House, watching the proceedings near the entrance was Charley Granger, the former Democrat from Harlem who retired last January after serving in the House for 46 years. Widely known on Capital Hill for his crafty mind and congenial manner, he was chatting with his successor, Andrew Espalier. "Thought I'd stop by and see the show," said Charlie in his characteristically gravelly voice. "You don't see history like this written every day."

"We sure did better than I thought we would."

"Yeah. Maybe too much better. You'd think not one of those tea partyers would have voted against Cain if he murdered his wife and kids. But every one of them —Garrett, Budd, Meadows, Weber, the others— voted to kick him out."

"I wonder why…"

Charley looked meditatively around." Andy, if Cain gets kicked off the stage, who stands to gain the most?"

"Vice"

"President"

"Rufus"

"Shilling. Mm hmm. Have you noticed how quiet he always is? Always standing in the shadows with a little smile on his rosy face while everyone around him is bickering and bashing their heads against each other. But he has the eyes of a snake."

"Before he became Vice President he was a televangelist, right?"

"Right. But beneath his charismatic Christian demeanor he's one of the conniviest bastards around. If he became president, his policies would be worse than Cain's, and his evangelical oratory would make everyone forget Cain's behavior in a weekend."

"Maybe you're onto something here."

"I wonder how many Republicans around here would like to see Shilling sitting in the Oval Office instead of Cain?"

Charlie bows his head in thought.

"Andy, something just clicked inside me."

"You don't say…"

"I'm getting a whiff of something. An odor that in all my years here I never smelled before. Shilling…I'd like to pry his evangelical head open and see what's inside." He eyes his watch. "Oops, my chauffeur's waiting outside."

"Well, good to see you again."

"Same here. If I have any more thoughts on this I'll get in touch with you."

"Okay. Maybe touch bases with Schumann up the road from us."

"Carl?"

"Yeah."

"Andy, that's a good idea. Being minority leader he has more power right now than any Democrat in the country, and being a senator he'll have a seat at Cain's trial. He could do some big things over there."

The *Article of Impeachment of the President* is now in the hands of the Senate as a subpoena that commands Conan Cain to be tried for high crimes he has allegedly committed against his country while in office.

During the initial proceedings, Democrat Faith Marron of Massachusetts spoke for many members when she said, "The President by committing his crimes has stuffed his pockets with millions of dollars that belong to the American people. But even these egregious acts pale compared to his traitorous betrayal of our nation to a dangerous global adversary. If he isn't convicted of his crimes as spelled in the *Article of Impeachment*, justice in this country will live as a sham and delusion in every moral mind in America."

But Republican Senator Hannibal Clow of Florida differed in what he saw was at stake. "The President's actions may deserve censure, but they do not rise to the level of impeachment, and any arguments to the contrary are vindictively partisan efforts to hound the President from office. Our government has no business intruding into anyone's private affairs; and if the President is convicted of these trumped charges, the Fourth Amendment of the Constitution, which states that every citizen has the right to be secure against unreasonable searches and seizures, might as well be repealed."

However, Senator Devereaux Irksen of Illinois brought every seat in the Senate to a hush as he rose to the height of his oratory powers: "Our citizenry is merely a tribe of animals, with animal instincts that will never be quelled. But the beauty of our enduring nation is that our forefathers hewed from the solid quarries of sober reason a way to sidestep our lower impulses and let our loftier powers lead us all together, as one, toward a collective prosperity that is far greater than could ever be the sum of our single parts. Yet one snare lies in this glorious path: When any citizen claiming concern for the general welfare strives against the common good. Of these enfeebling proclivities you know their names. Racism. Sexism. Antisemitism. Contra Latino. Any discrimination against those who differ from others in ways they can do nothing about, that under the anæsthesia of division and repression reduces the collective strength of our united citizenry. Whenever these inhumanities are detected —in any form— we, all of us as one, must unite and snuff this evil before it can weave its enfeebling spell; for enfeebling any one of us enfeebles all of us. By so uniting we each, weak or strong, rich or poor, fortunate or less so, can be the leaven in the bread of sociality that makes it rise to be the staff of life, and we each by our prospering deeds can lift the lives of everyone. So I say to those of our noble citizenry who would fall into that snare that lies in our path: Let our lower selves at times have their moments of pleasure. But never let those delinquencies obstruct our gathered numbers' aspirations to create a greater prosperity for us all."

Standing on the front steps of the House of Representatives, Majority Leader Wilson Gidea said, "We must draw this crucial matter to a close. But in doing so we must draw a line between right and wrong that is so clear that

WILLIAM HENRY HARRISON
PRESIDENT, MAR 4–APR 4, 1841

every child in America can see it. Some may say this trial signifies a sad day in America's history. But if we do what is morally right, this could be one of our brightest days, because we are adding the strength of our numbers to the strength of our nation's Constitution. With our deliberations, may the chilling wind of despair become a refreshing breeze of hope."

Yesterday evening CNN News reported that Vice President Rufus Shilling excitedly said to several of his colleagues in the Senate, "We have the votes, we have the votes!" to which one Senator replied, "Welcome, Mr. Future President. Soon you'll be cleaning up Cain's mess in time for the mid-terms."

From *The Washington Post:*
The President Is Acquitted of Impeachment

IN ONE OF THE biggest surprises in the history of American politics, yesterday the Senate voted to acquit President Conan Cain of all charges relating to Crimes he allegely committed as President.

For six weeks, the Senate deliberated behind closed doors until they had reached a verdict. Yesterday afternoon, the senators gathered in open session for the final roll call. With the whole world watching, the senators stood one by one to vote *yea* to convict or *nay* to acquit Cain of the crimes he had allegedly committed according to the *Article of Impeachment of the President of the United States*. The final tally: 49 *yea*, 51 *nay*, a robust 18 votes short of the 67 needed to convict. Of the 51 Republican Senators, 33 voted to convict and 18 to acquit; of the 49 Democrats, 16 voted to convict and 33 to acquit.

One would think the Republicans would have wanted to keep Cain *in* office, so why did so many try to vote him *out*? And the Democrats would have wanted Cain *out* of office, so why did so many vote to keep him *in*?

When Senate minority leader Carl Schumann was asked what may have happened, he provided the elemental clue. "Lately some Democrats began to wonder why so many Republicans were eager to remove Cain from office. I began to smell a rat from Montana. Then my crafty old friend Charlie Granger led me to the scent. He said that due to the mess Cain has made, many Republicans are so afraid the Democrats may win both houses during the mid-terms, they've conspired to convict Cain and move Shilling into the Oval Office in time to make everything look pretty before the voting booths open.

So the night before the vote," Schumann continued, "a quorum of Democrats convened for a very private meeting, and we decided we'd rather keep Cain *in* so the mess he made would keep scaring away voters rather than let Shilling rearrange the furniture before the votes were counted.

"Also, Cain has said if he's convicted he'll appeal the verdict, and though nothing like this has happened before, his Chief Counsel has described with the precision of a micrometer the grounds on which they could legally appeal. Cain also has a sleazy history of being sued and refusing to pay, then he wears the plaintiff down sometimes for years until they agree to take half of what they're owed then he doesn't pay them even that. He believes the key to winning is to never give in, so we decided to let him twist slowly in the wind until the voters can do what plaintiffs can't."

Asked if he thought what the Democrats did was unethical, Schumann retorted, "Unethical? We're doing nothing but bettering the instructions of the Republicans! Look how they illegally booted Gorsuch into the Supreme Court last year, and how they illegally gerrymandered many states' electoral districts after the 2010 census. Conservatives and Tea Partyers they call themselves. Crooks and thugs are better names. The real vote today wasn't whether to convict or acquit Cain, but whether our government's seekers of justice will all hang together or all hang separately."

Never was an ambush in the old west so craftily executed as this. From this cabal not the slightest clue leaked. Who knows what may next transpire, drip, drip, drip?

OVERHEARD ON CAPITAL HILL

WE'VE GOT TO kill him."

"After what he said before the elections about using the Fourth Amendment as an excuse to bump off Shillery, we could give him something he'd be familiar with."

"That would be too noisy. Even if we used a silencer, when he fell everyone nearby would look where the shot came from, and since he's guarded so securely the shooter likely wouldn't escape."

"So, we should do something that's quiet."

"Yes, and takes some time to sink in."

"Whatever you say."

"Maybe the less I say, the better."

Like a trap snapping, an idea springs in his head.

But he must think backwards.

From the committing to the conception.

From the last step to the first.

For surely, the perfect ending begins with a careful beginning.

For days, during every moment of eating, bathing, dressing, commuting, working, and every moment of repose, with evangelistic fervor his imagination scours his memory and wit for a clue. During every moment of dreamy slumber ions of subconscious thought steal through the tunnels of his brain..."

Finally pops the answer—at a moment he would have never suspected. While standing before a urinal and staring at the ceramic tiles before his eyes in a men's room on Capital Hill, the answer seemed to be scripted on the tiles...

'Each stab at his vitals would be small as a grain of dust.

'It would be quiet.

'And take time to sink in. Then I could be far away.

'I'll need a guidebook. And something to grind into powder.

'A jar? A baggie? In a pocket?

'But when?

'A dinner? I'd be as honored a guest as he. Little would he know that yon Cassius has a lean and hungry look.

'But the tasters?

'How would I get past them? Soup? Dessert? Salt? Pepper? Sugar? Keep thinking. Keep thinking. If need be, I can come up with a better idea.'

A WHITE HOUSE STATE DINNER

AT A STATE DINNER in honor of the visiting President of Argentina, dozens of diplomats, senators, husbands and wives convivially gather around a long linened table arrayed with settings of gleaming silver and bone china, President Conan Cain seated like a king at its head. A few yards away between the President and the kitchen door at his back lingers Vice President Rufus Shilling, his tall thin frame standing with his feet slightly apart and his hands clasped behind his back, looking for all the world like he's waiting to give a sermon, the kind he's given to audiences large and small. His snaky eyes beneath his fiery red hair dart right and left, keenly, observingly...

A waiter steps from the kitchen door carrying a plate of beef tenderloin and mashed potatoes and broccoli —opportunity! he steps forward— "Oops, excuse me."

"That's okay, sir," the waiter regains his balance.

"That the President's dinner?" eyeing the plate in the waiter's hands.

"Yessir," he glances over his shoulder at the kitchen door.

"If you have other things to do, I'll be glad to take it to him."

"Thanks, I forgot the gravy," handing the Vice President the plate.

As the waiter turns through the door, he holds the plate in his left hand close to his suit's right side pocket where his right hand swiftly lifts a scoop of powder, slips it beneath the potatoes, slips it in his pocket. As he carries the plate to the President seated in his chair he presses a floret of broccoli aside the potatoes.

"Your dinner, Boss."

As the plate slides in front of the President's tie he looks at the hand alongside to the face above. "Shilling."

"Things got a little crowded back there, thought I'd lend a hand."

"Always looking for something to do."

"I'm always looking for something to do. Truman once said vice presidents are as useful as a cow's fifth tit."

"Ha haa. He got to be president when Roosevelt died, right?"

"Yes sir."

"Heartbeat from the presidency, beautiful. If anything ever happened to me, the country'd be in good hands."

"That is an honor I would prefer to postpone for nearly eight years."

"Ha ha, I like you, Rufe."

"Thank you sir. Enjoy your dinner."

As the Vice President steps from the table the waiter steps from the kitchen door carrying a porcelain gravy boat. "Gravy, Mr. President?"

"Sure. More on the potatoes. I love gravy with mushrooms, beautiful."

The Vice President, his head bowed as if in prayer, strolls to a wastebasket in the corner of the dining room. Slips something from his suit's side pocket and drops it in. Coolly strolls from the room. Past guests milling in the hall. Through a door with MEN on it. Enters a stall and latches the door. As he leans over the bowl his right hand pulls from his side pocket a baggie of whitish powder and drops it in as his left hand presses the lever. The water rises in the bowl, the baggie sailing like a bubble on top, round and round, riding the delirious hem…descends into the maelstrom under his gaze…sinking…sinking —swoooshes into the drain. 'Nobody could *possibly* trace this.' An eternal gift from an absentminded God. He unlatches the door, leaves the stall, steps to a sink, turns on the hot and cold water, squirts liquid soap from the dispenser into a cupped palm. Scrubs his hands good and hard.

An SSA dressed as a waiter stands near the dining table. Out the tail of his eye sees a flash of something fall —like a spoon off a table. 'White House flatware? That's sterling silver.' He looks over. At the Vice President strolling from a wastebasket in the corner of the room. Trained to investigate anything unusual, he steps over. Looks in the basket. Crumpled napkins and other trash. 'What *was* it?' As if a Great Hand presses down on his shoulder he kneels and looks inside. Dips in his hand. Moves aside a few pieces of trash. 'I *know* I saw something.' His hand digs deeper. 'Feel silly doing this…'

…In the bottom of the basket between the trash and the basket's side, a stamped aluminum spoon with its bowl and handle bent into an L. "What's this?" mumbling. "Aah, piece of trash. Tossed it because it was bent." He looks away. 'Didn't look like it was stepped on or crushed.' He looks back…'Looks like somebody bent it into a little scoop.' He looks closer. 1 TBSP stamped on the handle. 'Why would somebody do that?' He stares. 'Maybe the guys at forensic would have an idea. If it's a piece of trash, they'll laugh their heads off.' The scales of curiosity tilt one way, the other…no…yes…no…yes…yes… no…yes… hesitantly, ooh so hesitantly, he reaches into his jacket side pocket and removes a sterilized baggie, 'You carry these forever and you never know when you might need one,' and slips his hand inside. Lowers his hand inside the baggie into the basket. Cups his hand inside the bag around the scoop. His other hand reaches inside the baggie and turns it inside-out until his first hand's thumb and forefinger outside the baggie pincers the scoop inside where the handle meets the bowl. 'If this is nothing but trash, I'll never hear the end of it.'

June 30, 2018, 8:26 am on CNN

WE INTERRUPT THIS PROGRAM to announce that President Conan Cain has taken ill. When he didn't get up for breakfast this morning at the usual time, he was found semiconscious in his bed apparently suffering from a gastrointestinal disorder. A physician on duty in the White House took his pulse and finding it erratic called an ambulance, and as a precautionary measure the President was taken to George Washington University Hospital less than a mile away, the same hospital that received President Ronald Reagen in 1981 after his attempted assassination.

Said the physician, "We found no cuts or bruises on his body, and after looking about the room we found no sharp objects or anything else that looked like it could be used as a weapon, so we suspect no foul play. We thought he might have gotten up in the night and fallen in the dark, but nothing was out of place in his room, and we found no evidence of anything like loose rugs or moved furniture. We also looked in the bathroom, and aside from a wet wrung washcloth on the side of the sink and a loose hand towel tossed on the back of the toilet everything was neatly in order there. We also found no blood in his stool, which eliminates a number of medical possibilities. We suspect he might have eaten something during dinner last night that didn't agree with him."

Until the President's illness is diagnosed, White House security has taken the precaution of cordoning the state dining room and the adjacent kitchen, locking every food served during the dinner the evening before in a walk-in refrigerator, and placing every article of kitchenware, silverware, and glassware used during the dinner in a vault. Every article of clothing the president wore last night has been preserved for examination.

June 30, 2018, 5:37 pm on CNN

We interrupt this program to announce that President Conan Cain is seriously ill. He is delirious and does little more than sleep, his pulse is weak, he occasionally suffers nausea and vomiting, and his kidneys and liver are functioning poorly. After extensive examination his physicians believe he is suffering from some kind of food poisoning. Since he ate nothing between leaving the state dinner the evening before and going to the hospital, the attendees sitting on his right and left at the dinner have been interrogated. They reported that the President ate the same food on the White House china that everyone else ate, that he enjoyed his dinner, and he displayed no signs of illness or discomfort or anything else unusual other than he didn't touch his pastry dessert. No one else attending the dinner has become ill.

At the hospital, doctors have taken blood samples as well as bone marrow and muscle tissue samples. Although when he arrived they routinely examined him and suspected nothing serious, they now are examining him for virtually every illness he could possibly have, even the chance he may have been "zapped" by something unusual from outside the White House. Every article of clothing he wore at the state dinner last evening has undergone forensic examining, but nothing suspicious has yet been found.

July 1, 2018, 7:02 am on CNN

Good morning ladies and gentlemen. President Conan Cain is gravely ill, and his doctors say he has been poisoned. Exhaustive medical tests reveal that the toxin was a species of mushroom known as *Amanita phalloides*.

Said Captain Edwin Klauber, head of the Presidential Protective Division, "Right now we believe someone tried to assassinate the President by poisoning him, who somehow administered the toxin orally. Our initial conjecture is it was administered while the President was eating during the White House state dinner two nights ago, and we first focused on the possibility that the poison may have been the mushrooms in the gravy served as the President ate his dinner. However, we have tested the gravy and the mushrooms it contained as well as every other food served at the dinner for contamination, including the salt, pepper, butter, and even the sugar and cream for the coffee served; and we found no trace of *Amanita phalloides* nor of any other poison.

"We also tested for any insecticides or herbicides that may have been sprayed on the vegetables, as well as any pollutants, industrial toxins, molds or bacterial decay that could have been on or in any other food that was served, and found nothing there. We inspected every piece of kitchenware, china, and silver used to prepare, serve, and eat the food; and we interrogated every person who had anything to do with delivering, storing, preparing and serving the President's food — all of which revealed nothing. We also analyzed the clothing the President wore for any allergenic or suspicious substances, and again found nothing. At this point, we can only pray that one step of discovery will lead to the next, until hopefully we can learn what happened."

Presently a team of doctors is working around the clock doing everything they can to save the President's life. His blood has been replaced with multiple transfusions, his digestive system has been decontaminated with volumes of liquid activated charcoal, he has been injected with large doses of penicillin and given fluids to rehydrate him, and since his liver and kidneys are not functioning he is on dialysis. He has a fever, his breathing is shallow, and his pulse is weak. The doctors say one reason the President's condition is so grave is that since White House security takes every precaution to make sure his food is safe to eat, they initially believed he merely had a mild gastrointestinal disorder. However, the period between ingestion of *Amanita phalloides* and the onset of symptoms is commonly six to fourteen hours, and during this time the victim often feels perfectly well while the lethal poison is insidiously entering the cells of the victim's liver, kidneys, lungs, heart, and nervous system. Hours later the victim begins to experience severe abdominal pain, diarrhea and vomiting, and by then some of his internal organs may be irreparably damaged. After a day or so the victim may believe s/he is feeling better, but by the third or fourth day the liver and kidneys fail and without intensive treatment the victim dies in five to ten days.

As for the poisonous mushroom, *Amanita phalloides*, the mature plant has a slightly crowned pale tannish-green cap usually about three inches across and a nearly white stalk about as thick as an adult's forefinger usually three to five inches long. The cap and stalk smell faintly sweet and taste rather pleasant, but every part of the plant is poisonous if ingested or even touched, and the dustlike spores are poisonous if inhaled. As little as half an average-size cap can kill a healthy adult, and the plant's toxicity is not reduced by cooking or freezing or drying.

Amanita phalloides typically grows around the trunks of hardwoods and conifers in moist areas throughout the temperate and boreal regions of North America as far south as Virginia. It blooms in summer and autumn, but in the southernmost regions of its range it may bloom in late spring. It occurs in dense woods in the Washington D.C. area, so Cain's would-be assassin could have found this poison locally this time of year.

At the White House and the Capital, everyone is praying for the President's speedy and complete recovery, and we at CNN ask everyone in America and around the world to pray for him also.

FROM *THE WASHINGTON POST*:
VICE PRESIDENT MAY HAVE POISONED CAIN

THE F.B.I. AND THE Presidential Protective Division, after making every investigative effort to solve the attempted assassination of President Conan Cain at a White House state dinner last June 29, have identified a suspect: Cain's trusted Vice President, Rufus Shilling.

While the President was eating dinner, a secret service agent dressed as a waiter observingly noticed Vice President Shilling drop a small object into a nearby wastebasket. As Shilling stepped from the room, the SSA stepped to the wastebasket and looking inside found a metal tablespoon whose handle and bowl were bent into an L-shaped scoop. He removed a sterile baggie from his jacket, slipped the scoop inside, and took it to a forensic laboratory.

Examination of the scoop found on the end of its handle fingerprints of

Vice President Shilling, on the bowl's inside dust particles of *Amanita phalloides*, and on the bowl's outside particles of mashed potato. This evidence points to the odious conclusion: Someone tried to murder the President during the state dinner of June 22 by grinding the deadly mushroom into a powder and mixing a scoopful into the President's mashed potatoes as he was about to eat —and that someone was Vice President Rufus Shilling.

Confronted with the evidence, with evangelical fervor Shilling denied knowing a thing about the incident, claiming he was somehow being framed for a terrible crime he didn't commit. At a press conference the next morning, with tears welling in his eyes Shilling passionately read a statement that said, "I swear before the Lord my precious saviour and redeemer that I had nothing whatsoever to do with committing this horrible crime against one of my closest friends and our beloved President. Due to my firm Christian faith I could *never* be tempted to do such a dreadful thing. As God is my witness, I swear I hadn't the slightest idea of this evil crime until the F.B.I. informed me of it."

The F.B.I. tried to examine the clothes the Vice President wore at the state dinner, but found that he had sent them to a dry cleaner early the next morning. The F.B.I. also examined Shilling's home including his kitchen and everything in it, and found nothing related to the crime. Yet one can only wonder: How could that scoop have Shilling's fingerprints on one end and particles of the poison and the potato on the other? And if he didn't do it, who did?

Still having no idea how this crime may have been committed, the F.B.I. returned to the White House and for the second time its agents interrogated every person who had anything to do with delivering, storing, preparing and serving the food the President ate at the state dinner.

When they questioned the waiter who was carrying the President's dinner from the kitchen to the dining room, the waiter mentioned something he hadn't thought of during his first interrogation. When he stepped from the kitchen with Cain's dinner, just outside the door the Vice President bumped into him slightly. The Vice President politely excused himself and offered to take Cain's dinner to him sitting at the dining table a few yards away, and since the waiter had forgotten the gravy he handed the President's plate to the Vice President and returned into the kitchen to get the gravy. "A minute or so later," the waiter said, "I returned with the gravy and poured some on the President's tenderloin and potatoes and also his broccoli."

"By piecing the evidence we have now," said Captain Edwin Klauber of the Presidential Protective Division, "we believe Shilling may have found this plant locally and ground it into particles and carried them and the scoop somewhere on his person, then he intercepted the waiter by the kitchen door and while taking the President's dinner to him sitting a few yards away he quickly slipped a scoop of the poisoned powder into the mashed potatoes. Since both were white," Klauber continued, "it would be hard to see the former in the latter. Even if someone did they might think it was salt, and since the poison tastes slightly sweet the President wouldn't have detected it as he ate his mashed potatoes covered with gravy. This would also explain how the poison may have been smuggled into the White House, since previously we had no idea how it could have gotten there." Klauber added, "Right now we have no other suspects, nor do we have any leads pointing to other possibilities."

Confronted with this new evidence, Shilling and his lawyers insisted someone else tried to kill the President and made it look like he did it. In a prepared statement Shilling's Chief Counsel proposed, "Since many people in this country strongly dislike Conan Cain and many believe Rufus Shilling due to his ardent politics would be no better a president, possibly thousands of people might think of committing such a crime as this. What a diabolically clever way this would be to get rid of two hated people at once!"

However, Attorney General Bricker Soliminus cautiously said, "Though we have no other suspects, we must adhere to the legal principle that in our system of justice, a person is innocent of a crime until proven guilty."

Though the Department of Justice is not completely sure that Shilling tried to kill Cain, millions of Americans are *very* sure. Sidewalks in front of government buildings everywhere constantly fill with clamoring pedestrians toting posters saying THROW SHILLING IN JAIL!, KILL THE KILLER!, and other slogans too distasteful to mention. If Shilling does so much as step from a limousine parked on a curb near an entrance a few yards away, crowds appear from nowhere and scream their outrage. Everywhere he sits or stands or eats or sleeps or walks, his aides prison him from every contact with the public while his mind holds in solitary confinement the stabbing fact of guilt.

In mind and body, many prisoners serving lengthy sentences in penitentiaries across the land are freer than he.

NBC NIGHTLY NEWS, 7:03 PM

GOOD EVENING, WELCOME to NBC Nightly News. This is Nancy Allison in New York. President Conan Cain continues to improve after an attempt to take his life two weeks ago. After he was poisoned a team of physicians worked around the clock for two days to save him from the very door of death. He was in a coma for three days and he still experiences headaches, irregular heartbeat, labored breathing, and occasional convulsions as well as muscular weakness and decreased coordination, and since his liver and kidneys aren't functioning he is connected to a dialysis machine. While he is convalescing, Vice President Rufus Shilling reportedly is faithfully executing the duties of the President. To learn more about how he is doing, let's go to the White House. Vice President Shilling, are you there?"

"Yes, I'm here," his rosy face and fiery red hair looking elegantly cheerful as his tall lean figure is seated behind the Oval Office desk.

"Good evening Mr. Vice President, welcome to NBC news."

"Thank you Nancy, good to see you again."

"So, how are things going in your surrogate role as President?"

"Fine. Yes, excellent."

"Is the work challenging?"

"Well, yes, of course. But in the President's absence, my firm Christian faith provides me the strength to devotedly carry out his policies in his behalf and in behalf of the American people. We live in a dangerous world, and in his absence we mustn't let our guard down for a minute."

"What do you think of the F.B.I.'s continued efforts to do everything they can to discover who may have possibly tried to kill the President?"

"Oh, I support them in every way. They must unceasingly search for the

152

perpetrator of this terrible crime until they find him."

"What do you know about the waiter who says he gave you the dinner plate to take to Cain's table?"

"Only what I read in the newspapers. I personally have no recollection of anything like that happening. Possibly when the waiter was questioned a second time, in the interrogators' zeal to learn what happened, a zeal I applaud by the way, perhaps the waiter was so pressured he finally said what the interrogators wanted to hear even though he thought it might be untrue. But I am only guessing."

"Who do you think could have possibly committed this crime?"

"I can think of many possibilities, minus one."

"You have refused to take a lie detector test regarding this incident. Can you tell us why?"

"I would be glad to. Every time I think of this terrible crime, I get…" he bows his head, purses his lips, wipes the corner of his eye, takes a deep breath, "and —and the kind of anxiety I experience is the kind of response that often registers as a lie on such a test. So if I took such a test, it might say I was lying when I was really telling the truth. Also, during a lie detector test, the interrogator often mentions some of the objects that were at the scene of the crime, then watches how the suspect reacts. Since by now I've read so many articles about what happened that evening, with the result that I have become familiar with everything that occurred at the crime, if I took such a test, certain details I remembered from reading the newspapers might seem like details only the perpetrator would know about."

"Like a small scoop?"

"Like –uh –but –what scoop?"

"The scoop found at the crime?"

"I –I don't anything about a –scoop –spoon whatever it was."

"But you just said you have become familiar with everything that occurred at the crime."

"Not– uh– I'm afraid you didn't understood what I said."

"If you were familiar with everything that occurred at the crime, why wouldn't you be familiar with the most important evidence discovered there?

"I –uh –what are you getting at?"

"Maybe you don't know what I'm getting at, but I think our audience does."

"I believe your audience knows that due to my firm Christian faith I could *never* commit such a horrible crime. This has upset me very deeply."

"How might the perpetrator have ground the powder?"

"Ah– I– no, what powder. I hope Cain is feeling well."

"Do you ever imagine being in the mind of the person who committed this terrible crime, and wonder how he must feel about the agony he has caused the President to endure for possibly the rest of his life?"

"I –uh –no, yes, my firm Christian faith provides me the strength to de-votedly carry out the President's policies in behalf of the American people. My thoughts go to his family who have grieved terribly during this unfortu-nate ordeal, as have I. God bless America."

"Thank you Mr. Vice President. Thank you very much."

From *The Washington Post:*
President Cain is Removed from Office

WASHINGTON— According to the American Constitution, Amendment 25, Section 4: *Presidential Vacancy, Disability, and Inability*, at noon yesterday Conan Cain was officially removed from office as President of the United States and has been succeeded by Vice President Rufus Shilling.

Since Cain's attempted assassination six weeks ago, he has been slowly recovering. With extensive therapy his doctors say he may improve somewhat, and a year from now he may be eligible to undergo kidney and liver transplant surgery. However, the effects of Amanita poisoning are permanent, and after lengthy observation and neurological testing his doctors believe he will never be as mentally and physically capable as before. In addition to being con-nected to a dialysis machine he walks with the aid of two canes, he often slurs his speech, his writing is somewhat scribbly, he usually looks like he's about to fall asleep, and he repeatedly says, "I can't play golf anymore."

American Constitution Amendment 25, Section 4, says in part, "Whenever the Vice President and a majority of the principal officers of the executive departments believe by written declaration that the President is unable to discharge the duties of his office, the Vice President shall immediately assume the duties of the office as Acting President." If the President objects, a situation known as *contested removal*, Congress has three weeks to debate the issue, then a two-thirds majority of the House and Senate is required to remove the President. After this decision there is no appeal.

After President Cain's doctors advised that he be removed from office, the following events transpired…

☞ On August 13, Vice President Shilling and a majority of the President's Cabinet spent the morning with President Cain during which they discussed government affairs. Concluding the same as Cain's doctors, they sent to the Speaker of the House of Representatives and the President pro tempore of the Senate a written declaration that Conan Cain is no longer able to perform his duties as President of the United States and should be removed from office, signed by the Cabinet members who observed him as well as Cain's doctors.

☞ On August 14, President Cain objected to being removed from office.

☞ On August 15, the House and the Senate began debating the issue.

☞ On August 21, the House voted 412 to 3, with 16 abstentions, that President Cain is unable to perform the duties of his office.

☞ On August 22, the Senate voted 93 to 0, with 7 abstentions, that President Cain is unable to perform the duties of his office.

☞ At 12 noon August 23, 2018, President Conan Cain was officially removed from office and Vice President Rufus Shilling was sworn to succeed him in the Oval Office before Chief Justice John Glover Roberts. Rufus Shilling is now the 46th President of the United States.

Much of the public believes that Conan Cain has gotten what he deserves, with one night show host saying, "President Cain had a hard time filling high-ranking government positions, including the highest."

But much of the public believes that Rufus Shilling has gotten anything *but* what he deserves —that in their eyes exists the ocular proof of the unforgiveable crime this so-called evangelical Christian has committed.

From the sandy coasts of California to the rocky coves of Maine, with the quickness of a struck match crowds of Democrats and Republicans alike often gather along public sidewalks, in shopping malls, on college campuses, even at local athletic events where the usual public annoyance at political sloganeering has become a cheering entertainment, and they clamor in hopes that something can be done to redress the grievances that sear their souls. Residents mount Anti-Shilling signs on their lawns. Businesses display them in their storewindows. Vehicles everywhere brandish Anti-Shilling bumper stickers. The President becomes the subject of scorn by nightshow hosts, the butt of crude locker room jokes, the onus of condemnation by the media, an exemplar of sin in church sermons —and the expression "committing a Shilling" fast becomes an idiom for viciously betraying a friend.

A common expression of discontent is to splatter government buildings with grenades of feces. One hurler proclaimed, "Even America's dogs and cats have found a way to express their disgust at the President."

The latest Cantor poll indicates that public opinion of Shilling has plummeted to single digits. It seems the nation has become an angry mob that would hang the man with the fiery hair and snaky eyes from the nearest tree if they could lay their hands on him. And the F.B.I. never finds another suspect.

With evangelical fervor Shilling urges the F.B.I. to keep looking for Cain's attempted assassin until the person is found —but he and his lawyers obstruct the pursuit of justice at every turn, blackening truths with shadows of doubt that may seem consummately communicative to Shilling but are the epitome of disgust to the public. At a televised press conference Shilling's Chief Counsel said, "The F.B.I. is investigating the motives of the secret service agent who said he retrieved a scoop from a waste basket in the White House dining room. We have only this person's word that he found that object where and how he claimed. We urge the F.B.I. to examine this person's professional and personal background for any clue that might possibly suggest he would betray our country for material or psychological gain. We are doing our own investigating," the attorney went on, "and we have reason to believe the agent may have the kind of criminal mind that would lead him to use his stature as an agent of the law to conceal a serious crime he committed."

The F.B.I. vehemently denied they were investigating the secret service agent who found the scoop. Director Clarian Valley stated, "In the professional manner in which he with almost clairvoyant perception carried out his assigned duty, he displayed the highest integrity expected of an officer of the law; that if anything, he should be acclaimed as a hero. Except for him, President Cain's attempted assassination may have gone down in history as one of the greatest unsolved crimes of the age. Now having to endure the additional insult of slander, the agent should be further commended for his courage in the face of undeserved adversity."

Newspapers nationwide branded the Chief Counsel's statement as criminally false on its face. *The Omaha Star* proclaimed, "President Shilling and his legal accomplices are using our government as a shield to avoid being punished for a horrible crime he has committed. Worse, they set a depraved example that murder may be a useful way to try to succeed in one's work."

The Honorable Valerie Backman Bonnett, Chief Judge of The U.S. District Court of Michigan, said of the Chief Counsel's statement: "When a lawyer perpetrates a fraud upon the court during testimony, he is committing a crime for which he should be disbarred. Similarly, when Shilling's Counsel perpetrates a fraud upon the court of public opinion, he is committing a crime for which he should be disbarred. Anyone who would paint a surely innocent man in such criminal stripes commits a serious crime that aligns with the crime of the accused, and public opprobrium should be heaped upon him."

Reverend Hector Williamson, president of the Evangelical Fellowship of America, said, "Our new President —it smites my conscience to state his name— is the vilest of hypocrites. When he cites his Christian faith as proof that he would never kill our president, he is the Devil cloaked as an angel, and his sham evangelism is an insult to devoted worshippers everywhere."

Natalie Tammar, a young mother from Kingston, Illinois, expressed the sentiment of millions when she said, "It makes me cringe to think that an attempted murderer is President of the United States!"

In the halls of Capitol Hill, members of Congress shun him. In New York the United Nations all but declares him off limits. Abroad, the usual visits of a new American President with foreign heads of state do not occur, typically with such insinuations as, "Our Chancellor, or President, or Prime Minister, is presently too occupied with serious domestic issues to entertain America's new president." Members of the judiciary don't know what to do with him. On one hand they "know" he has committed a crime for which he should severely punished; yet the Constitution says only "If the President [meaning Cain] is unable to discharge the duties of his office the Vice President shall succeed him." And everyone in the Department of Justice knows if they "push too hard" to push the President out of office they might be pushed out of their offices. As has happened before in the halls of politics, as the scale of justice balances morality against duty, it often has a spineless fulcrum.

In every session of the House and Senate, every effort President Shilling makes to clean up President Cain's maladministrations before the midterms only dirties them even more. Every bill he tries to pass is mockingly voted down by Republicans and Democrats alike, each member fearing any association with him will woo away their constituents in the fiefdoms they represent.

One Congressional effort of Shilling is particularly shunned: his attempt to appoint a Vice President. No matter how consummately communicative his every effort may seem to him and his closest advisors, each appears as detestable to Congress and the public. House Minority Leader Nandra Pelosa of California and House Minority Whip Sorian Hoyle of Maryland issued a joint statement saying, "All too well we remember two years ago how the Republicans obstructed President Obama's effort to appoint a Supreme Court Justice near the end of his term. How presciently they revealed then how every member of conscience in Congress should act now: to similarly obstruct appointing a Vice President of Shilling's choice near hopefully the end of his term."

This final sentence portends a momentous omen for the nation's President: If during the midterm elections the Democrats gain a firm foothold in the House and Senate, these bulwarks of democracy will clamor to convict Rufus Shilling for the high crime of attempting to assassinate a President.

Is this a prediction of the future —or the dream of a fantasist?

A "Discovery" Trial

FACING THE WINDOW overlooking Lafayette Square, Hod aims the cane at the White House beyond. Waves its tip up down right left…

"…I'll say it for the thousandth time, I did not do it."

"Well theyen, who deeid do it?"

Hod mumbles, "I'd know that Texas drawl anywhere. Summerland."

"I have no idea. That's why I keep urging the F.B.I. to continue searching for the perpetrator. But apparently they're getting discouraged."

"I'm gettin discouriged too. 'Cause evera time I xpect to get a pat on the back from my constituents I get a kick in the ass, and if this keeps up I maight not get alected. And I'm not the only Republican who's wurried bout this. If you don't turn this around re-al soon, we all gon' suffa. If the Dems win big in both houses this fawl, know what they'll do?"

"I've thought about it."

"Well, you betta think about it re-al hard, cause the first thing they gon' do is impeach you. Then you can pick your poisin: resign or be removed."

"I pray every night for a more peaceful resolution."

"Whatever you do, don't play the Christian card, it makes people laugh."

"I worry about that too."

"Well, it's time for me to go."

"Thanks for stopping by, Ormond."

"Rufe, I'll say it again. If you did this, you can buy only so much law with the prizes of your crime."

—**SMASH!** —the door behind Hod shatters into splinters and its top slams onto his back and throws him on the table which overturns toward th window as a SWAT team pours through the door. "What the hell!" yells SWAT 1 as he stands over Hod sprawled in a tangle of wires and a cane and a recorder and a clipboard and a cup of spilled coffee. SWAT 2 and SWAT 3 step to SWAT 1's sides as SWAT 4 steps around the overturned table to the window while SWAT 5 guards the door.

SWAT 1 leans over Hod on the floor. *"What the hell you doin boy!"*

SWAT 3 kneels and looks at his face. "It's an old man!"

SWAT 1: "I don't give a shit what he is, *what are you doing here?*"

"What's it to you?"

SWAT 1: "It's a goddamn lot to me NOW WHAT ARE YOU DOING HERE?"

Hod covers the back of his head with his hands.

SWAT 1 looks around Hod's body. Sees the cane with the cords dangling from the handle. "What's this?" picking it up. "Feels heavy in the shaft." He whacks the end of the cane hard on the edge of the overturned table —pieces of electronics fly everywhere. *"What the hell you doing with this!?"* he yells, looking at Hod sprawled on the floor.

SWAT 4 looks out the window. "Look. The White House."

SWAT 1 aims the remains of the cane at the window. "Son of a bitch!"

They all gather around Hod lying on the floor. SWAT 1 leans over him and yells in his face, "For the twentieth time, *what are you doing here!*"

"Wouldn't you like to know."

SWAT 1: "You're damned right I would like to know! Bill, see what else is here. Don't step in the coffee you dummy!"

SWAT 3: "A little tape recorder. It's plugged into the cane. It's running."

SWAT 1: "No kidding! Well, hit the rewind button. Okay, hit play."

"... First thing they gon' do is impeach you. Then you can pick your poisin—"

SWAT 1: "That's Summerland, Senator Summerland."

"... I pray every night for a more peaceful resolution."

SWAT 2: "Shilling's voice!" Hey, I think we found the guy! After all these months, we finally found him!"

SWAT 2: "Jeee-sus. We thought it'd be some peachfuzz cybersleuth."

SWAT 3: "So much for social profiling!"

SWAT 2 sets the chair back up and two men jerk Hod off the floor and shove him onto the chair.

SWAT 1: "Now for the thirtieth time, what the hell are you doing here?"

Hod pouts. Rubs the back of his shoulder where the door slammed into him. Feels the side of his bruised face.

SWAT 1: "Quiet guy eh? Cuff him and search him!"

As one man uprights the table two men grab Hod by the armpits and jerk him to his feet and cuff his hands behind his back and search his pockets. On the table appear some keys. Wallet. Ballpoint pen. Bills and coins. SWAT 1 grabs the wallet and opens it. "Hod Hawksbill your name?"

Hod pouts.

SWAT 1: "Charlottesville Virginia where you're from?"

Hod pouts. Tries to rub the side of his bruised face on his shoulder.

SWAT 1: "Okay Mr. Hawksburg or Hawkskill whatever's your name, let's go! Bill, gather everything here and label and bag it and bring it to the station!"

FROM *THE WASHINGTON POST*:
"DEEPER THROAT" IS EXPOSED

WASHINGTON— The mysterious person who has secretly been taping conversations occurring in the White House Oval Office since President Conan Cain was inaugurated in January 2017 has been found. He is Hod Hawksbill, a journalist who worked in Washington for more than forty years before he retired in 2007 to Charlottesville, Virginia.

For well over a year the Secret Service has searched everywhere around the White House and the Capital for someone it believed was recording conversations of President Cain and President Shilling in the Oval Office and on Capitol Hill. Their search finally ended on the third floor of the Hay-Monroe Hotel north of Lafayette Square. While looking out a window facing the Square and the White House beyond, Hawksbill would aim an aluminum cane whose shaft contained a powerful digital antenna and voice recognition software programmed to detect Cain's or Shilling's voice, then he would tape their conversations with a recorder plugged into the top of the cane.

No one suspected an elderly man limping on a cane to be the notorious scribe who documented the conversations of two sitting Presidents. Several times during the Secret Service agents' extensive search, they encountered this person on the streets and in the cafes around the White House and Capital Hill. Each time they ignored him as a suspect.

Clay Cockspur, the President's Press Secretary, praised the Secret Service's unending efforts. "Month after month they never gave up looking for this secretive mole, who destroyed the reputations of two of this country's finest civil servants, who contributed to the attempted murder of a President and all the suffering he will endure for the rest of his life, and who continually publicized classified information in a manner that has harmed millions nationwide. On behalf of the American people, we believe there are not enough days left in eternity to adequately punish this evil beast for his wicked crimes."

FROM *THE WASHINGTON POST:* THE BEAST, KISSED, BECOMES A PRINCE

WASHINGTON— In response to the White House's condemnation of Hod Hawksbill yesterday concerning his recorded conversations of Presidents Conan Cain and Rufus Shilling, *The Washington Post*, rather than argue with the White House's conclusions, has decided to take its argument to the people by posting on YouTube all of the 76 "Smoking Gun" tapes Hod Hawksbill recorded of the two Presidents' conversations that are presently archived at *The Post*. Then everyone around the world can decide for themselves whether Conan Cain and his cronies, individually or severally, should be universally praised or universally condemned.

Contrary to Mr. Cockspur's denunciation of Hod Hawksbill, *The Washington Post* believes Mr. Hawksbill and his taped conversations have performed an indispensable service to the American people in the manner in which these actual conversations have exposed the serious crimes Presidents Cain and Shilling routinely and willfully committed while pretending to serve the public, which together constitute the most evil misuse of power by any president of this nation since its inception nearly a quarter of a millenium ago.

We can only congratulate Mr. Hawksbill on his brave and patriotic "keyhole diplomacy", and we wish him well in the future.

DEMOCRATS WIN BIG IN BOTH HOUSES

WASHINGTON— As every poll in the nation had predicted, in the midterm elections yesterday the Democrats gained majorities in both the House of Representatives and the Senate. In the House the Democrats gained an impressive 64 seats, tilting its numbers from 194 Democrats and 241 Republicans to 258 Democrats and 177 Republicans. Percentagewise, the Democrats increased their seats in the House from 44 to 59 percent.

In some ways the Democratic gains in the Senate were more significant. They gained 13 seats, increasing their numbers from 48 to 61, decreasing the Republicans' numbers from 52 to 39. Now that the Democrats hold at least 60 percent of the Senate, if their party acts as a bloc they can control the selection of Supreme Court Justices.

In both houses the Democrats now can set the agenda of legislation for the next two years. No doubt they will be extremely busy —to borrow a phrase— "making America great again" by repairing the maladministrations of Cain and Shilling, restoring the moral integrity of our government, and repealing Cain's legislation as fast as he endeavored to repeal the legislation of President Obama before him.

Many Republican candidates who lost were faced with explaining to their constituents why they so ardently supported two Presidents who continually committed serious crimes. In these respects, one could say these candidates rode the Presidents' coattails out of office.

One noteworthy trend in these elections is that in a number of gerrymandered districts previously controlled by Republicans, they lost due to extensive voter registration in these districts' largely democratic urban areas combined with dissatisfied Republicans in outlying areas.

Democratics also made big gains in the nation's state elections. They gained six governorships, increasing their numbers to 22 of the 50 states; and they retook eight legislatures, now a majority of 26 of the 50 states.

From Travis Simmile's Night Show

THIS IS **TRAVIS SIMMILE**. Welcome to our show. Tonight we have with us Hod Hawksbill, recorder of the Smoking Gun tapes that brought down two American Presidents. Since Cain was inaugurated in January 2017, Mr. Hawksbill taped 76 conversations between Presidents Cain and Shilling and their conspiring cronies. Since they were posted on YouTube several months ago, millions have listened to them worldwide. After the mid-term elections last November, the tapes influenced the House and Senate to subpoena former President Conan Cain's tax records, reopen the Department of Justice's investigation of Cain's global businesses which he used the Presidency to stuff millions of dollars into his pockets, and impeach President Shilling for attempting to assassinate President Cain on June 22 of last year. During the last few weeks Mr. Hawksbill has appeared on nearly every TV news program and night show around the country. Tonight we are happy to welcome Mr. Hod Hawksbill."

Applause...

"Welcome Hod."

"Good to be here, Travis." Hod settles in the sofa beside the host, a T-handled aluminum cane resting by his side.

"So how does it feel to be famous?"

"About the same as when I was secretly leaking information to the press back in the Seventies and Eighties."

"I understand you attended many of President Lyndon Johnson's press conferences back in the Sixties."

"Yes I did."

"That's half a century ago. And you leaked information to the press during every presidency from Nixon to the second Bush, right?"

"Actually, everyone but Ford. He didn't do much worth reporting."

"Ha haa...so you knew the ropes when you taped Cain's conversations."

"I knew what to look for and why it was important, and what the public had a right to know."

"How do leaks work?"

"Pretty much the way a leaky faucet works. Drip, drip, drip."

"Ha haa … so how did you obtain your leaks and who'd you give them to?"

"I usually obtained them from insiders working for senators and congressors on Capital Hill. Each time I would write an article about the information I obtained, then send it to *The Washington Post* and other newspapers mostly on the East Coast. Who I leaked it to depended on what the information was about and what was the newspaper's editorial policy."

"I see. How important are leaks?"

"The media couldn't serve the public justly without them."

"Are leaks really ethical?"

"They're more ethical than the covert activities of corrupt officials who would exploit the public for their own personal gain."

"So, when you leaked such information to the press, you believed you were being ethical by acting in the best interests of the public."

Right. You could say it was a necessary evil that enabled the public to know about the corrupt forces that make up the swamp."

"The swamp. You found a lot of swamp in Washington this time around."

"More than ever. Even Nixon was drained land compared to Cain."

"Drained land. So you could say your tapes helped to drain the corruption in Washington known as the swamp."

"Yes. To extend the metaphor, you could say they helped create a solid ground of integrity, open for all to see, that enables the public to understand how their elected government officials are representing them fairly."

"I suppose the tapes vary a lot."

"Mmm, yes and no. They usually have a bad political smell, but beyond that the information can be almost anything."

"The Senate subpoenaed a number of your Smoking Gun tapes to use as evidence in President Shilling's impeachment trial, correct?"

"Correct," Hod grins. "I gladly complied."

"I bet. Altogether, you taped 76 conversations?"

"I taped a few dozen more, but they didn't say anything worth listening to."

"Tell us how you taped those conversations……"

SOMEWHERE NEAR CHARLOTTESVILLE

WHO WOULD'VE THOUGHT it could happen!" says the little man in his lair as they chat about the new administration in Washington.

"A woman president!" says Hod.

"Nandra Pelosa. Has a happy hop to it, doesn't it?"

"She sure hopped into the Oval Office after the midterms when the Dems gained big majorities in the House and Senate."

"From Minority Whip to Speaker of the House to President. Happens when there's no Vice President after the President vacates office."

"Wonder what our forefathers would have thought?"

"Wonder what Shillery thought?"

"Yeah. I bet she won't be ironing her pantsuits anytime soon."

"How about Shilling? After he resigned he left town like he was riding a missile."

"But the law will catch up with him. A federal judge has already indited him for trying to kill Cain."

"He won't be preaching on television anytime soon."

I don't know about Pelosa though," Hod laughs a little, "appointing two lawyers hardly out of grad school to the Supreme Court after Ginsberg and Breyer resigned."

"Things could be worse."

"Thinking of worse, how about Cain? He'll probably lose a few billion bucks by the time the feds finish shaking his pockets, and the only real estate he'll probably own will be a doghouse with a dialysis unit inside."

"At least he'll be eligible for Medicare."

"In a year, he may be eligible for liver and kidney transplants."

"He'll be a candidate again."

"His children also might be living in a few doghouses next door, hopefully hooked to dialysis units that remove waste from their consciences."

"Their hands were as filthy as his."

Hod looks contemplatively around the room. "If someone ever wrote a

166

book about this, what would you want it to say about you?"

"Nothing! Absolutely nothing! I don't want anybody to know my name or where I live! I know what I've done, and no one can take that away from me. If there's a Heaven up there, I'm sure Somebody'll have a nice place waiting for me someday. What more could I want?"

"That would be the height of success for anyone."

"But I wouldn't mind getting to know that fellow better who taped all those conversations in Washington. Seems we'd make an enchanting match."

"Ha haa!" Hod slumps on the stool before the counter against the wall piled with computers and has a good laugh.

"If I met him, maybe we could do some interesting things together."

"If I run across him, I'll see what I can arrange."

"I'd appreciate it. Because I do have something else we could work on."

"Ooh? What kind of encore are you cooking up?"

"Mmm…maybe doing the same with the so-called "democrats" and "liberals". In addition to mending all the damage Cain has done, get them to shrink the bureaucracy, and outlaw gratuities to lobbyists and excess contributions to election campaigns, and increase taxes on large incomes and end deposits in offshore accounts, and understand that some day our government is going to have to start living within its means, and a list of other goodies for my beloved abstraction, the American people."

The little man looks around the room. At the keyboards and wide-screen displays in front of him. At all the computers piled against the wall on his right. At the long row of product catalogs at his back and the wall above paved with notes. At all the other items scattered about that have played a wondrous role in his glorious labors. He contemplatively nods.

"Our work is only half done."

NOTES

1. "Donald Trump's Conflicts of Interests: A Crib Sheet": Jeremy Venook, Apr 7, 2017, *The Atlantic* [page 93].
2. "From Russia with Oil": Yonathan Zunger, Mar 26, 2017, *Medium Daily Digest, A Medium Corporation* (an online publishing platform) [page 103].

POLITICAL CARTOONS

ACKNOWLEDGEMANTS

First I thank Jim Phillips, a retired journalist who worked for many years in Washington, D.C., who told me much about the political scene in Washington and vetted every part of this novel for political accuracy. To him this book is dedicated.

I thank my wife, Janis Butler, for enduring my inattention to all other aspects of our lives while I was penning these pages.

I thank my dog, Gilly. Time and again I would be so mired in words that the more I tried to disentangle them the sloggier I got —then Gilly would nudge the back of my chair. My thoughts shattered, we'd go outside and she would reset her bladder controls and check the premises for trespassing coons and possums, then when I returned to my typed words I was productively refreshed. But for her, this book might have taken months more to write.

www.ingramcontent.com/pod-product-compliance
Lightning Source LLC
Chambersburg PA
CBHW060330260626
47160CB00007B/2745